Whaler
'Round the Horn

by Stephen W. Meader

THE BLACK BUCCANEER

RED HORSE HILL

AWAY TO SEA

LUMBERJACK

WHO RIDES IN THE DARK?

T-MODEL TOMMY

BOY WITH A PACK

CLEAR FOR ACTION!

BLUEBERRY MOUNTAIN

SHADOW IN THE PINES

THE SEA SNAKE

THE LONG TRAINS ROLL

JONATHAN GOES WEST

BEHIND THE RANGES

RIVER OF THE WOLVES

CEDAR'S BOY

WHALER 'ROUND THE HORN

BULLDOZER

THE FISH HAWK'S NEST

SPARKPLUG OF THE HORNETS

THE BUCKBOARD STRANGER

GUNS FOR THE SARATOGA

SABRE PILOT

EVERGLADES ADVENTURE

THE COMMODORE'S CUP

THE VOYAGE OF THE JAVELIN

WILD PONY ISLAND

BUFFALO AND BEAVER

SNOW ON BLUEBERRY MOUNTAIN

PHANTOM OF THE BLOCKADE

THE MUDDY ROAD TO GLORY

STRANGER ON BIG HICKORY

A BLOW FOR LIBERTY

TOPSAIL ISLAND TREASURE

KEEP 'EM ROLLING

LONESOME END

THE CAPE MAY PACKET

Whaler 'Round the Horn

Stephen W. Meader

ILLUSTRATED BY EDWARD SHENTON

LITTLE ROCK, ARKANSAS
www.southernskies.com

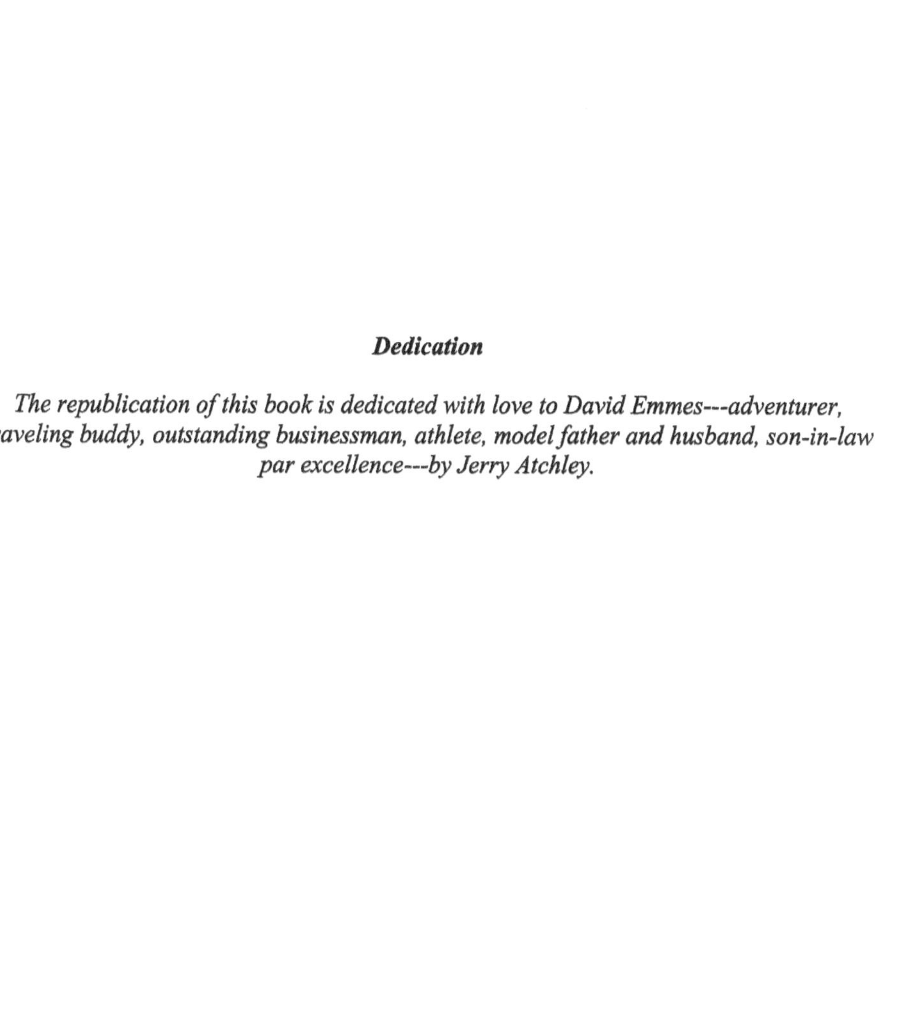

Dedication

The republication of this book is dedicated with love to David Emmes---adventurer, traveling buddy, outstanding businessman, athlete, model father and husband, son-in-law par excellence---by Jerry Atchley.

Foreword

A HUNDRED YEARS AGO on the New England coast, a boy with adventure in his heart looked upon whaling as the most glamorous of vocations. The sperm whale fleet out of New Bedford alone numbered between four and five hundred ships, and many men made fortunes out of whale oil and spermaceti.

Youngsters who had the proper seamanship and daring might become mates at 18—captains at 20. More than one of them retired, comfortably well-to-do, before his thirtieth birthday.

Such men were the exceptions. Thousands who sailed before the mast died in battle with the monsters they hunted, or lived to crippled old age without saving a penny of their small wages.

It was a hard life, but it held moments of such glorious combat as could be found in no other calling on land or sea.

For seventy years the Yankee whalers dominated every ocean. Then, with the suddenness of catastrophe, the industry collapsed. Two things happened to it. One was the wholesale sinking of whale ships by Confederate cruisers during the War Between the States. The other, an even more damaging blow, was the discovery of petroleum in Pennsylvania. Cheap oil took the profit out of the whale fishery.

A thoughtful young man came home from years of whaling and beachcombing in the Pacific to write a story that has become a world-wide classic. His name was Herman Melville and his book was *Moby Dick*.

I cannot hold with the idea that *Moby Dick* is properly a boy's story. It has a grandeur and sweep in many of its passages that compare with Shakespeare's tragedies or the Book of Job. And it contains a wealth of allusion that makes its greatest appeal to a mature reader.

In *Whaler 'Round the Horn* I have tried to catch the thrill of whaling and the magic of the Pacific islands with no attempt at the impossible task of rivaling Melville. It is my hope that many of the teen-agers who read my story will be led to a fuller enjoyment of *Moby Dick* and *Typee* as they grow older.

I wish to express my appreciation to Dr. Wendell C. Bennett, Yale University anthropologist, whose researches in the valley of Kalalau have been exceedingly helpful in the development of the story; and to Mr. Charles Fern, publisher of the *Garden Island* newspaper, who showed me the wild beauty of Kauai.

Stephen W. Meader

*Whaler
'Round the Horn*

I

A MUD-SPATTERED traveling chaise, pulled by a gray horse, came down the rutted road through the pines, rumbled across the wooden bridge and stopped a few yards from the boat landing.

Young Rodney Glenn, sculling his dory up-channel with the flooding tide, looked curiously at the carriage. He had good eyes but he didn't recognize either the horse or the driver. The turnpike from Boston and Newburyport to Portsmouth ran farther eastward and it was an unusual thing to see strangers traveling on this little-used stretch of road.

It was a mild afternoon for January, but the sea wind came in sharp across the tide flats. Rod blew on his hands and put more power into the single oar. As he shot the dory neatly alongside the rickety landing stage the man in the chaise hailed him.

"Ahoy there, sailor," called a deep, cheery voice. "What water is this? And what town?"

"Great Bay," the boy replied. "Town o' Durham. State o' New Hampshire."

He made fast the painter and started heaving his catch to the dock. There were half a dozen cunners, averaging perhaps a pound apiece, and close to a peck of clams.

The man got out of the chaise and stretched his legs as if they were stiff. The horse stood wearily, head drooping.

Rod grinned. "You must've come quite a piece," he observed.

"Left Kennebunk this morning," the stranger answered. "Any place around here that puts up travelers?"

"There's a tavern at Dover an' one at Newmarket," said the boy. "But they're pretty far for a tired horse."

"Well, I'm not too fussy," the man smiled. "Suppose your folks could find me a place to sleep?"

Rod looked him over while he made up his mind.

The stranger was a strong-looking, ruddy-faced, bearded fellow of thirty or thirty-five. His clothes were well-cut and of fine material. But what the boy liked most about him were his eyes, blue and steady, with little crinkles at their corners. He walked with a slight roll, like a seafaring man.

"Trouble is," Rod replied, at length, "my uncle an' aunt are away. They went to Portsmouth for the night. Don't know what they'll say, but I guess it's all right if you're willing to sleep in my bed an' eat my cooking."

The man's head went back in a lusty laugh.

"My boy," he said, "that's what I call real hospitality. I accept. And if you'll lead the way, we'll find out what sort of a cook you are."

Rod put the fish and clams in an old canvas bag and slung it over his shoulder.

"Come on," he said. "It's only a couple o' hundred yards down the road."

They entered the bleak dooryard and stopped before a weather-beaten little gray-shingled house. Lilac bushes, leafless now, flanked the granite doorstep. Beyond, connected to the house by a closed shed, was the barn.

Rod opened the leather-hinged, double barn doors and the stranger drove the chaise inside. They unharnessed in silence. When the horse was stabled, the boy brought water from the pump in a wooden bucket and pulled down an armful of hay from the loft. Then he picked up the man's portmanteau.

"All right," he announced, "we can go in through the shed."

The kitchen of the farmhouse was warm and fragrant.

"Is that beans I smell?" asked the traveler. He sniffed the air gustily and with obvious delight.

"Yep," Rod replied. "I've had a pot in the oven all day. Do you like chowder?"

"Wonderful!" the man chuckled. "Just give me a knife and I'll open the clams."

While he took the succulent littlenecks from their shells, Rod cut up potatoes and onions and crisped some bits of salt pork in the skillet. A kettle was steaming on the stove, and into it he put the potatoes, onions and pork to boil. The milk was heated in a separate pan, and the boy added a generous chunk of butter. When the potatoes were soft he told his guest to put in the clams. And a moment later he poured the buttery milk into the kettle, finishing with salt and pepper and a double handful of Boston crackers.

"Ah!" breathed the stranger, his nose close to the rising steam. "Pure ambrosia! A feast for all the gods on Olympus! You're a master cook, lad—I can see that, and smell it, too!"

Dusk had fallen when Rod ladled the concoction into bowls. He lighted a whale-oil lamp and they sat at the pine table and ate chowder and baked beans till they could hold no more.

At last the traveler leaned back with a benevolent smile. "Fifty leagues I've come for this," he said dreamily. "For this and the sight and smell of the sea. All the way from Lenox, in the Berkshires. A fine place, filled with philosophers and poets and talk —talk—talk. Never turn writer, my boy. You'll be talked to death. You'll lose the good, salty freshness of living."

"You—you're a writer?" Rod asked in awe.

"Trying to be," the stranger answered lightly. "It's hard to say if I'll ever succeed. My true calling is that of a world-voyager. Even now my feet are restless for decks and ratlines."

The boy's sober face lighted up. "You mean you've been to sea?" he asked. "Before the mast?"

"Yes. I've been in many fo'c'sles. I've shipped as sailor and whaler. I've been a castaway on islands where cannibals bask under palm trees and the soft trade winds are forever blowing."

"Gosh!" said Rod.

The man glanced at him keenly. "I take it that you, too, would like to follow the sea," he said.

"I guess I'd rather be a whaler than anything else in the world," Rod answered firmly.

The stranger looked at him without a word for a full minute.

"Hm," he murmured at last. "You'd be willing to freeze in the rigging in a Cape Horn wester? You'd eat salt horse and moldy biscuit? You'd pull your heart out to get fast to a whale and risk your neck under the crash of his flukes?"

"Yes," Rod replied without hesitation, and the man nodded as if he understood.

"Strange," he said, "that the most dangerous of all trades, and the poorest paid, should make such appeal to brave hearts. But I'm with you, boy. I know the feeling."

"I've talked to Uncle Eli," Rod blurted. "He knows how much I want to go to sea, but he calls it foolishness. He's a farmer—not a sailor like my father was—an' he thinks I ought to stay on dry land. I don't aim to spend all my days hoeing an' clamming. Those islands in the South Seas—I've dreamed about 'em nights! An' I guess the quickest way to get to see 'em is aboard a whale ship."

The man across the table smiled. "Quickest?" he said. "Yes, if you can call a three-year voyage quick.

But you're right—the merchant clippers don't stop at the island ports. They used to call at Honolulu or Hilo for sandalwood, but that trade's about done. It's the whalers that crowd the island harbors now. When do you plan to start?"

"Soon as I can get away. I'm 'most seventeen an' used to boats. I'd make a better 'foremast hand than some o' these upstate clodhoppers."

The stranger nodded. "How badly do your uncle and aunt need you?" he asked.

"They don't need me at all," said Rod. "It's a small place—only eighty acres an' four cows. Sometimes they claim I eat 'em out o' house an' home, but I reckon the work I do an' the fish I catch pay for my keep. If I left tomorrow they wouldn't really miss me."

"What time do you expect them home from Portsmouth?"

"Not before noon tomorrow. Why?"

"Oh, I was just thinking," said the man. "I might be able to give you a lift. I'll be going to Boston on my way back to Lenox. From there you could get to New Bedford without too much trouble, and there'll be plenty of whalers in port, readying for voyages."

Rod had been listening, openmouthed. He stumbled to his feet and groped his way to the door.

"I've got to milk," he said huskily. "Maybe I'll have my mind made up when I come back."

He lighted the tallow candle in a pierced tin lantern and by its dim light made his way out to the barn. The stranger's words still rang in his ears. "Whalers in port, readying for voyages . . . islands where the soft trade winds are forever blowing."

It was warm in the tie-up, close to the cows. He milked them methodically, one after another, and bedded them with straw. Then he put a measure of oats in the gray horse's manger and brought the two brimming pails of milk into the kitchen.

The stranger had tidied up. The pots and dishes were washed and put away. He was whistling softly to himself and he eyed the boy shrewdly but said not a word.

Finally Rod could stand it no longer. "All right," he burst out, "I'll go with you! We'll start soon as I've done the morning milking, an' I'll leave a note for Uncle Eli."

The bearded man smiled a little and shook his head.

"Poor lad," he said softly. "There'll be times when you'll hate and curse me for this. What you'll find is sweat and suffering and mighty little return for your pains. And yet—if you're like me, as I think you are—no power on earth or sea can keep you from going a-whaling. It's settled, then. Show me where I'm to sleep. We'll be off in the morning."

Rod gave the traveler his own bed, up under the eaves. For himself he chose a spot in the corner of the kitchen and rolled up in a quilt on the floor. For a long time he couldn't sleep. The decision he had made involved the most important change in his life since the day he had been left an orphan and come to live on his uncle's farm. He knew Eli Glenn would resent his going to sea, yet he was sure in his heart that he was right and that the crusty old farmer was wrong.

Hours later he crawled out of his quilt, lighted the lamp once more and brought pen, ink and paper from the cupboard. The words of his message had already formed in his mind. He wrote quickly, in a firm hand:

"Dear Uncle Eli and Aunt Louisa:
"When you read this I will be a long way from here. I am going to ship aboard a whaler. All I am taking is my clothes and the four dollars I earned picking blueberries. I figure they belong to me. I am leaving my father's silver watch because I might lose it or get it stole. Some day, if I come back I would like to have it. The cows have been milked and the pig fed. There are some fish I caught in the cold box in the shed. Yrs. resp'y, Rodney."

Long before the winter sun came up, Rod had started a kettle of mush boiling over the fire and done the morning chores. When he came in from the barn the traveler was in the kitchen, his portmanteau packed and his beaver hat and blue traveling cloak laid ready on a chair.

They ate their mush and milk in silence. Then Rod put a chunk of rock maple on the fire so that it would keep, and placed the note he had written beside the clock. He put on his old reefer-jacket.

"I guess we're ready to go," he said.

Ten minutes later the horse was harnessed to the chaise and they were on the road. With each mile that dropped behind them, Rod felt a growing elation. He was free—starting his great adventure. The bearded stranger seemed to share the feeling. He told story after story of his own whaling experiences, in words so vivid that the boy sat spellbound. He could feel the swaying crosstrees under his feet—see the deck far below and the vast circumference of blue— hear the breathtaking cry of the lookout, "Blows! Ah, blows! Thar she blo-o-ows!"

The stranger brought him back from his daydreaming with a matter-of-fact statement.

"New Bedford's where you'll want to go," he said. "When I shipped for my first voyage, Nantucketers were kings of the whale-fishery. You could hail

Nantucket ships on all the seven seas. But the old Quaker skippers are dying off or retiring, down there. They never did have good anchorage. New Bedford's the port now—with three or four hundred whalers sailing every year."

"Seems as if I can't wait to get there," Rod murmured.

"That's all right," the man smiled. "But don't sign on with the first ship you see. Ask some questions first around the taverns and chandlers' shops. You see, there are bad captains and good ones—lucky ones and poor, unfortunate fellows that couldn't raise a sperm whale's spout in a whole year's voyaging."

The horse jogged on through Exeter, then down the road to Hampton. After a long day's traveling they reached Newburyport just at dusk. The stranger offered to pay for Rod's lodging at the inn, but the boy preferred to sleep on straw in the stable, where grooms and drivers were accommodated free. It was late afternoon of the second day when they sighted the spires of Boston through the haze.

Rod, who had never been to the city before, stared in awe at the tall buildings, at Faneuil Hall and the famous Old North Church.

"We'll dine at the inn yonder," said the bearded

man. "Then our ways part, for I have friends that I must visit here."

He bought the boy an excellent meal and they sat talking for a while when it was finished.

"I'm working on a book," the traveler said, "a story of strange experiences." He paused, a faraway look in his eyes.

"Is it about whaling?" asked Rod eagerly.

The stranger seemed not to hear for a moment. Then he shook himself like a man coming out of a trance.

"Yes," he answered grimly. "It's about the greatest of all sperm whales, and the most terrible. It's about the white whale himself. And if, in your wanderings, you should encounter that whale, may the Lord have mercy on your soul."

Rod was still under the spell of those words when they left the inn. The man drove him down to the warehouse section, where freight wagons were loading for the south. One of them, piled high with bags of wool and pulled by a four-horse team, was just about to start.

"Ahoy, driver!" called the traveler. "Where are you bound?"

The freighter looked down at him sourly and spat over the wheel. "Don't know's it's your concern," he drawled, "but I aim to git to New Bedford 'bout this time tomorrer night."

"Fine," laughed the bearded man in the chaise. "Got a passenger to ride with you. Here—catch!"

He tossed a silver coin up to the teamster and motioned to Rod to climb up among the bags.

"I wish you better luck than I had at the whaling, lad," he said, as he shook the boy's hand. "Look me up some day when you get back. There'll be those, I hope, who'll have heard of me by then. And if my book sells, the world will be more respectful of whalers."

Rod thanked him and started to climb on the wagon, then thought of something.

"Wait," he cried. "I don't even know your name."

The man chuckled deep in his beard and touched the whip to the gray horse.

"Call me Ishmael!" he shouted over his shoulder.

II

THE NIGHT wind off the harbor had a bite in it, but Rod burrowed down among the bags of wool and was snugly protected from the cold. Even the jouncing of the wagon over the cobbles was eased by the soft material on which he lay. Soon he dozed off and slept soundly all through the night.

At daybreak the wagon pulled into a tavern yard for a change of horses. The teamster shoved the butt of his whip into the boy's ribs and woke him.

"Git up, if ye want any breakfast," he growled. "We won't be here more'n twenty minutes."

Rod scrambled out of his nest and ran to the inn kitchen. A plate heaped with ham and eggs and a mug of hot tea cost him fifteen cents. It seemed like a good deal of money but he was in no position to argue. By the time the driver came out, wiping his mustache on the back of his hand, the boy was back on top of the load.

That was a long day. The horses plodded steadily through woods and farmland and there was no view of sea or hills to break the monotony. The driver was a grumpy individual, disinclined to talk. Left to his own thoughts, Rod had a few pangs of conscience. At first he had been half hypnotized by the glamorous traveler in the chaise. Now he began to feel sorry for his uncle and aunt. Perhaps he had been a bit hasty in leaving as he did, but it was too late to turn back now. He was bound to try his fortune among the whalers.

His first view of New Bedford, through the gathering dark, was a disappointment. It didn't look like much of a town. But a moment later, when he caught a glimpse of the forest of masts along the waterfront, his spirits rose once more.

The grumpy driver's tongue loosened a little, now that the journey was over.

"Got any place to sleep?" he inquired.

"No," said Rod. "I'm a stranger here. I guess there are inns that'll put me up, though."

"Suit yerself," the man shrugged. "But I reckon ye ain't too well fixed fer cash. Ye're welcome to stay here on the wool. There's nobody here to unload, this late, an' I don't want to hang around all night watchin' it."

"I see," the boy replied, grinning to himself. "Sure, I'll be glad to stay with the load. Thanks."

The man led his horses off to their stable, and Rod settled down among the bags. It was probably a softer bed than he would find in any waterfront tavern.

It grew colder in the night, and a few flakes of snow fell. The boy was stiff when he slid down from the load at daybreak. He considered his guard duty done and set out to hunt a breakfast.

A walk of two blocks along the snowy street brought him to a small inn that bore a swinging sign, "Harpooner's Rest." The signboard was hung from the shaft of a rusty harpoon. Peering through the small-paned window he saw a light inside and pushed open the door.

The floor was sanded and a smell of stale liquor hung about the dark wood bar and tables. A sleepy-looking, gray-haired man was puttering about, wiping the tables with a rag.

"Are you serving breakfast yet?" asked the boy.

The old fellow nodded. "Fish chowder's all we got, but plenty o' that," he replied.

Rod sat down and watched the barkeep ladle out a huge bowl of the steaming stuff. It wasn't as good a chowder as he could make himself, but it was hot and nourishing. He finished the bowl and had a second helping, then put the pewter spoon down.

"Many whale-ships in port?" he asked, trying to sound casual.

"Usual number—twenty or thirty, I reckon," said the old man. "Cap'n Cory brought in the *Louisa* yesterday—out three years an' two months. Good v'yage, though. She's got twelve hundred bar'ls, most of it prime sparm."

"I suppose there are some about ready to sail?" Rod continued.

"Shouldn't wonder," the barkeep replied. "You a whaleman?"

The boy's face reddened. "Well, I—I aim to be," he stammered. "I'd like to get with a good skipper."

"Hm-m," said the gray-haired man, squinting at his customer. "O' course the best ones don't have to take greenhorns, if that's what you be. Good seamen sign aboard their ships. But there's young Cap'n Jonas Beale, startin' his first v'yage in command. He was first mate o' the *Prudence,* an' they say he's a prime whaleman. Maybe he's still lookin' for hands."

"What's his ship?" Rod asked eagerly.

"The old *Pelican,* Nantucket-built. Nothin' fancy, but new-rigged an' sound-timbered. She's made six or seven v'yages, all pretty lucky. Ye'll find her down at Long Wharf."

Rod paid for his breakfast and left the tavern. In five minutes he was strolling along the wharves that lined the Acushnet River. High bowsprits jutted upward over the cobbled roadway, and masts and rigging made a complicated pattern against the pink sky of sunrise.

Life was beginning to stir along the waterfront. A drayload of empty oil casks came rumbling down the street. A tipsy-looking sailor stumbled out of a grogshop and sat down suddenly in the gutter, a bottle still clutched in his hand. Right beside Rod, a ship chandler opened the iron shutters of his dingy little store.

"Good morning," the boy greeted him. "I'm looking for Long Wharf and the *Pelican.* Can you tell me where they are?"

The man jerked his thumb to the left. "Down that way a couple o' cable lengths," he answered. "Aimin' to sign on for the voyage?"

"I might," said Rod. "What kind of a skipper has she got?"

"Young Beale? Good man, I'm told. He ain't but twenty-three or twenty-four, but he's been whalin' for ten years. He's a driver—works his crew hard. But he's a fair man. I know there's good grub aboard —sold him some of it myself. You could do a lot worse'n the *Pelican*."

That was all the encouragement Rod needed. He set off at once in the direction the ship chandler had indicated, and soon found himself looking up at the carved figurehead of the ship he sought. Most of the other vessels had gilded torsos of women at their prows. For this one the figurehead maker had chiseled out a big bird, wings spread backward in flight and huge, pouched bill resting on its breast.

"What's the matter, Bud?" asked a voice at his shoulder. "Do you think to see her fly?"

He swung about and saw a lad a little younger and smaller than himself, freckle-faced and grinning. The boy's blue eyes held a mischievous twinkle, and he had a good chin and a wide, generous mouth.

"Just admiring the work o' the artist," Rod replied. "You know anybody in the *Pelican's* crew?"

"I'm one," said the boy proudly. "It's my second voyage. Seth Norton, seaman, that's me."

Rod put out his hand. "Howdy, Seth. My name's Rodney Glenn. Where'd be a good place to find your captain?"

"He sleeps aboard," young Norton answered. "All the supplies are loaded, an' we're waiting for a fair wind an' a good tide. If he can ship a couple more hands I reckon Cap'n Beale might sail 'fore night."

As they walked out along the wharf toward the waist of the ship, Rod saw a face appear at the rail. The man looking down at them was hardly more than a boy himself, but tanned and muscular-looking. A blue cap with a visor was tilted back jauntily on his curly brown hair.

"That's him now," Seth whispered. "That's the skipper!"

Rod gulped, then gathered his courage. "Captain Beale," he asked, "could you use a foremast hand?"

It was hard to tell what the captain was thinking as he sized him up.

"Come aboard and let's have a look at you," he said finally.

The young skipper was standing by the break of the poop when Rod and his companion reached the deck.

"Ever been to sea before?" he asked.

"Not in a ship. But I've been rowing and sailing small boats all my life."

"How old are you?"

"Seventeen, come May."

"Where from?"

"Durham, in New Hampshire. My dad was mate on a ship out o' Portsmouth, before he died."

Captain Beale looked him up and down. "Take off your jacket," he said. "Let's see how you're built."

Rod whipped off the heavy reefer and squared his shoulders.

"You look strong enough, and quick," the captain nodded. "Maybe you can pull an oar and we can teach you to hand, reef and steer. I've seen worse greenies turn into pretty fair whalemen. I'll give you a two-hundredth lay. Come in the cabin and sign the ship's papers."

Marveling at his good luck, Rod followed the skipper of the *Pelican* down the companion ladder. On the table in the snug cabin was a log book in which he signed his name. Many other signatures filled the page above his own—some of them strange-looking foreign names, some mere crosses. One was a crude drawing of a turtle.

"All right, Glenn," said Captain Beale, sprinkling sand over the ink to dry it. "We'll be sailing with the evening tide. Bring your dunnage aboard by eight bells o' the afternoon watch."

The boy's face glowed with pleasure. "Aye, aye, sir," he replied smartly, and climbed to the deck again.

Seth Norton was waiting for him on the wharf.

"How'd it go?" he asked. "You signed on? What lay did he give you?"

"Guess I'm going to be your shipmate," Rod grinned in reply. "I'll get a two-hundredth lay. What's yours?"

"Hundred-an'-fiftieth," the freckle-faced youngster replied. "Yours is fair enough for a lubber, though. Nobody ever gets rich out of a whalin' voyage except the owners, an' maybe the cap'n an' mates."

Rod stepped back to get a better view of the ship. He had never looked at a whaler before. The *Pelican* was no greyhound of the seas, it was obvious. Her bows were broad and bluff, and her bowsprit thrust upward at a steeper angle than those of the clipper-built ships. There was nothing unusual about her rigging, but all three masts looked thicker and stronger than in a merchant vessel. The most noticeable difference was the queer brick structure that rose from the deck amidships. In reply to Rod's question, Seth explained that this was a try-works.

"You'll find out how it's used, first time we get fast to a whale," he said. "Makes quite a sight at night. You'd think the whole ship was afire."

They left the wharf together.

"Where's your dunnage?" asked Seth. "One o' the taverns?"

Rod was a bit embarrassed. "All the dunnage I own is what I've got on," he said. "I came from Boston on a freight wagon an' slept last night on the wool bags. I do have a few dollars, though. Think I ought to buy some things?"

Seth laughed. "Shucks, no!" he said. "Anything you need you can get from the ship's stores an' charge against your pay. Look—why don't you come home with me? My folks live right handy here."

Rod said he didn't want to put the Nortons to any trouble but Seth was insistent. After a walk of a few blocks they turned into a side street, overhung by the bare branches of elms, and went around to the back door of a comfortable-looking frame house. They wiped the snow off their boots on an iron scraper and entered the big, warm kitchen.

"I've brought a new shipmate home with me, Mother," Rod heard his young friend saying. "Thee doesn't mind, does thee?"

A kind-faced woman in a simple gray dress and starched apron looked up from the piecrust she was rolling.

"Not a bit, Seth," she answered with a smile. "Thee knows I like to meet thy friends."

Rod wasn't surprised to hear the "plain language" of the Quakers. He knew New Bedford was largely

a Quaker town, and many members of the sect had
prospered in the whale fishery.

Shyly he shook hands with Seth's mother. His
mouth watered at the pleasant smell of baking that
came from the oven. Looking about he saw two
younger children staring at him. A girl of eight or
nine was peeling potatoes and a smaller girl, with
yellow pigtails, was solemnly eating bread and jam.
The sticky stuff was smeared on both her plump
cheeks. He grinned at her and she ducked behind
her mother in a sudden access of bashfulness.

"Come on up to my room, Rod," said Seth.
"Dinner won't be ready for a spell, an' we can get
acquainted."

The New Bedford lad's bedroom was large and
sunny and it had a pleasingly nautical look. In one
corner Rod saw a coil of hempen whale line and
a carefully polished harpoon. On a table was a
whale's tooth, bigger than a man's fist, and a two-
foot model of a full-rigged ship, complete to the last
brace and halyard.

"I brought back the tooth from my first voyage,"
Seth explained. "Father built the little ship. He was
a whaleman, too. First mate o' the old *Walrus*. But
he lost an arm in a fight with a big bull whale off the
Seychelles. That was in 'thirty-eight—twelve years
ago. He came ashore an' started a rope-walk, an'
he's done right well with it.

"He's a part owner o' the *Pelican*," the boy added proudly. "One-twelfth share. He supplied all her cables an' cordage an' whale line."

By noon Rod was on as good terms with his new friend as if he had known him for years. They had told each other the stories of their lives, and the liking they felt was mutual. The New Hampshire lad realized how lucky he was to have discovered an experienced whaler near his own age who could show him the ropes.

Mr. Norton came home for the noon meal. He was as cordially friendly as his wife had been, and Rod felt at ease among them from the start.

"Better eat hearty, young man," the elder Norton told him. "These are likely the last home-cooked victuals thee'll have for many a day. From what I hear, Jonas Beale's ready to sail with tonight's tide."

"Eight bells, he told us," said Seth. "That's four o'clock, Rod. We'd better leave here by three."

Well before that time he had his small sea chest packed, putting in an extra shirt or two and a pair of dungarees for Rod. Seth's mother didn't cry when she bade her son farewell, but she hugged him close, a tenderness in her eyes such as Rod had never seen.

"I'll be praying for thee, my little Seth," she

whispered. Then she glanced toward the other boy and must have seen what he was feeling.

"For thee, too, Rodney," she said. "May the Lord bring both of you safe home."

They didn't say much as they carried the chest between them down to the wharf. But the sight of a crowd of people gathered on Long Wharf loosened Seth's tongue.

"Look there!" he exclaimed. "They've warped the *Pelican* out already. See where she lies in midstream? That means the cap'n's ready to make sail."

They hurried toward the group on the wharf. Rod saw Mr. Norton there, and Seth's two small sisters. Other families stood with them, come to see their men off. And there were half a dozen sailormen with sea bags and chests.

"Not much time for good-byes," Mr. Norton told the boys. "Here's the second mate now, to take you off."

At that moment a red-bearded head appeared over the edge of the wharf and they were startled by a roar like a bull's bellow.

"Come on, ye spalpeens! What are ye tarryin' for? Tide's turned. Into the boat wid ye now an' make it lively!"

III

THAT'S Mike Flynn, the second mate," Seth murmured hastily. "He's a driver. We'd better hustle."

They tumbled into the whaleboat, along with others of the *Pelican's* crew who had been on the wharf. The craft was loaded nearly to the gunwales when the men at the oars pushed off.

"Spring, ye tigers!" howled the red-haired mate. "Put yer backs in it!" And almost before the New Bedford lad could wave good-bye to his father and sisters, they shot out across the running tide.

A moment later, Rod was scrambling up a rope to the whaler's deck. To the accompaniment of a running fire of orders, the boat was swung up to the davits and made fast.

Captain Beale's voice rang out calm and clear from the quarterdeck. "Send 'em aloft to make sail, Mr. Flynn. And man the windlass. Get that anchor up an' catted."

A dozen men went scuttling up the shrouds to take their places along the yards. Prodded by a belaying pin in Flynn's hands, Rod ran forward, grabbed one of the capstan bars and began heaving in the anchor chain, in company with a broad-backed Negro and a couple of Portuguese seamen. Hardly had they lifted the heavy anchor to the bitts when great squares of canvas broke out aloft and were sheeted home.

The boy felt the movement of the deck beneath his feet, as the ship heeled a little to the quartering breeze and picked up speed. Under topsails and topgallantsails, she took her stately way down the river. And a cheer, coming faintly from the distant wharves, sped her on her voyage.

Rod had little time to relish the thrill of his first sailing. Along with Seth and the other late-comers he was ordered below to stow his dunnage in the forecastle. It was a dark, narrow, smelly place, with bunks along the sides and a greasy table in the middle.

A whale-oil lantern swung in gimbals overhead and gave a feeble light. The only berths not already occupied were far forward, close to the head. Seth shoved his sea chest under the lower bunk, and Rod took the upper one.

"They'll call us back on deck to pick watches, pretty quick," said Seth. "I'll try to get you in the same watch with me, so I can help keep you out o' trouble. Flynn's pretty tough on green hands. I hope we get in the first mate's watch."

They heard a hail, "All hands on deck," and went up the companion ladder. Twenty-five or thirty men were gathered there, around the foremast foot.

"Here come the officers," Seth whispered. "That tall one's Ezra Macomber, the first mate."

Rod saw a lanky, stoop-shouldered man with gray whiskers moving forward beside Mike Flynn.

"All right, boys," he said quietly. "Line up across the deck so we can get a look at ye."

They formed a ragged line and the choosing began. The majority of the crew were able topmen and whalemen, and it was natural that these should be picked first. As each man was called out he went to stand behind the mate who had selected him and the choosing went on, turn and turn about. Seth, as he had hoped, was picked by Macomber.

Now there were only nine or ten left in the line,

and all were obviously green hands, awkward and ill at ease. Flynn scowled at them and finally pointed to a big, lumbering farmer lad. Rod, who had been trying to make himself inconspicuous, drew a breath of relief. He saw Seth whisper something to the tall first mate.

"You," said Macomber. "Third from the left, there."

Rod hesitated an instant before he realized he was being called out. Then he sprang forward with alacrity. As he reached Seth's side, the New Bedford boy gave him a triumphant wink but said nothing. The choosing went on till all the remaining men and boys were assigned watches. Each mate gathered his group around him.

Rod could hear the rough voice of Mike Flynn laying down the law to the starboard watch.

"An' get this," he bellowed. "I'll bash the head o' the first wan o' yez that don't jump when I give an order!"

Macomber's attitude was more reasonable. He spoke quietly and earnestly.

"Some of you are old hands," he said. "You know what's expected of you. I don't aim to be too hard on you others till you've got your sea legs. But there'll be no loafing in my watch. You've got to learn fast, an' I expect the able seamen to teach the greenhorns. With good luck we'll be on whale grounds inside a month, an' by that time every man of you has got to be a sailor."

Darkness had nearly fallen now, and the sails loomed ghostly above them as the ship stood out toward the heads.

"Take a last look at the land," Seth told Rod. "We aren't likely to see it again till we raise the Azores or the Canaries."

A mournful voice called them away from the rail. "Po-o-'t watch!" it sang. "Come an' git it!"

By the forecastle hatch a thin, wrinkle-faced Negro stood with a steaming bucket in his hand. With Seth to guide him, Rod hurried to get his pannikin and stood in line to have it filled.

Like most ship's cooks, the lean old man went by the name of "Doctor." He had a word for each man he served, old acquaintances and newcomers.

"Eat hearty, boy," he told Rod. "Las' fresh grub you'll git fo' a long, long time."

The food in the pannikin turned out to be fish chowder, rich with chunks of cod and halibut. It was steaming hot and properly seasoned, and the boy ate it with a good appetite.

Four bells rang as he finished, and while the starboard watch went to get their supper, Macomber's men took the deck for the second dog watch.

The tall mate sent a couple of hands aloft to set staysails. Then he turned to Seth Norton.

"Take the wheel," he told the boy. "Keep her sou'west, a point west, an' give thy young friend here a lesson in steering."

They were out in Buzzards Bay now and the wind was freshening. Seth gripped the big wheel, keeping his eye on the binnacle. The *Pelican* had begun to pitch and roll in a beam sea and the youngster had his hands full holding her on course.

"I heard the mate say 'thy' when he spoke to you," said Rod. "Is he a Quaker, too?"

"Yep, he's a Friend, an' so's the skipper. Asa Tetlow, the cooper, is another. Then there's Mose Howland and Rufe Coffin—both on their second voyage. We've got 'most as many Quakers aboard as we have Portygees. We Friends are mighty peaceful folks, but we can sure fight whales."

Rod watched his struggles with the wheel, his fingers itching to grasp the spokes.

"How about it if I helped?" he asked. "Maybe I could start learning."

"All right," Seth replied. "Take hold on that side an' turn whichever way I tell you. There's a trick to it. You've got to guess one jump ahead to hold her on course. If you wait till she falls off an' then try to pull her back you'll be zigzagging all over the ocean."

Rod soon discovered what he meant. There was an amazing kick to the wheel when a sea caught the rudder. Seth watched the oncoming waves out of the corner of his eye and tried to spin the wheel just enough to allow for their force. The compass needle under the binnacle light swung from side to side, but Rod could see that its average direction was never more than a point or two from the course the mate had ordered.

"This weather isn't so tough," Seth panted. "In a real gale o' wind it takes two good men to steer. All we've got now is a good breeze."

Rod was grateful for the exercise that kept him warm, for the northwest wind bit right through his heavy reef-coat and wool shirt. At the end of an hour the first mate came by and glanced at the binnacle with approval.

"Good steering," he grunted. "I'll send Manuel aft to take the wheel, an' the two of you can go for'ard on lookout. Keep an eye to loo'ard. We ought to be off Penikese Island by the end o' the watch."

A broad-shouldered, swarthy Portuguese, with silver rings in his ears, came back along the heaving deck and relieved them at the wheel. In a moment or two Seth and Rod were perched in the fore shrouds, peering out over the sea to the southward. It was a good time for talk.

"Just so you'll get the hang o' things," said the New Bedford boy, "I'd better tell you about the afterguard. You've seen the cap'n, an' the first an' second mates. Most whalers carry four mates—one for each boat. Our third is a Portygee named Sanchez. Pretty fair whaleman an' a first class topman. The fourth is Injun John. He's only part Injun an' a lazy kind of sailor, but you ought to see him lance a whale!

"Then there are the harpooners—boat-steerers, we generally call 'em. They're a cut above the crew. They berth aft, in the steerage, an' when we're in whaling waters they spend most o' their time aloft in the crow's-nests. A queer enough bunch you'll find 'em, too.

"The chief mate's harpooner is a Kanaka from the Sandwich Islands. Smiling Jimmy is the name he goes by. In Flynn's boat there's a great big Negro called Lucifer. Old Matty Gage steers for Injun John, an' the fourth mate's harpooner is a real Injun —a Gay Header named Tedeconk. He goes around half-naked most o' the time, an' has a turtle tattooed on his chest. That's the way he signs his name to the articles—with a picture of a turtle.

"That's all o' the afterguard except the sailmaker,

the carpenter, who's an old Nantucketer, and Asa Tetlow, the cooper. He works on the barrels an' casks, an' forges harpoons."

Rod, staring into the night, thought he saw a flicker of white, far to leeward. "Look," he said. "Is that a line o' surf?"

Seth looked where he pointed. "Breakers!" he sang out. "Two miles to loo'ard on the port bow!

"That'll be Penikese," he told Rod. "We're moving right along. Ought to be sighting Cuttyhunk Light any minute now."

They picked up the flashing yellow light a short time after, and when four bells struck they were nearly abeam of Cuttyhunk Island.

As the starboard watch came scrambling on deck, Seth greeted Rufus Coffin with a grin. "You fellows are just in time to go aloft," he said. "They'll give the order to wear ship, soon's we're clear o' the shoals."

Rod accompanied his friend below and prepared to turn in. The forecastle was close and foul-smelling after the clean air on deck. Two greenhorns from the starboard watch were seasick and still lay moaning in their bunks. Rod had paid little heed to the ship's motion until now, but the heaving and rolling seemed to be worse in this cramped space. With a squeamish feeling he pulled off his boots and jacket and crawled into his berth.

He had hardly closed his eyes when heavy feet came clumping down the ladder. Flynn's big voice fairly shook the bulkheads.

"Tumble out, ye pair o' lubbers!" he roared at the seasick men. "Spring, now, or I'll flog the hide off ye!"

Terrified, they staggered to their feet and made for the companion, the rope's end in the mate's fist swishing around their legs. It was rough treatment for sick men, but it made Rod so angry he no longer thought about the reeking forecastle and the tossing of the ship. He turned toward the dark side of the bunk and in a few minutes he was asleep.

At midnight a hand shook his shoulder and he started up so suddenly he bumped his head against a deck timber. For a moment he sat there bewildered, unable to recall where he was or how he got there. Then a shout brought him back to reality.

"Roll out, there, ye loafers! Eight bells! Port watch on deck, an' lively!"

Rod struggled into his boots and jacket, pulled on his wool cap and joined the knot of men swarming up the ladder. The cold sea air struck him as he emerged on deck, clearing his head and soothing the uneasy feeling in his stomach.

The *Pelican* was running before the wind now. Looking aloft, he saw that topsails and courses were squared away, and the pennon at the mizzen peak blew straight forward.

"We're somewhere south o' the Vineyard," Seth told him. "Can't see the shore in the dark, but she lies off there to port. The old hooker's footing right along. We'll be clear o' Nantucket by sunrise."

The watch passed quietly enough until the last hour. Then, shortly after six bells, there was a shift in the wind. It came suddenly, falling first to a calm that let the sails droop and the stays go slack. Mr. Macomber barked out a sharp order to man the braces, and almost before Rod could get his hands on the rope there came a gust from the southwest, heralded by a great slatting of canvas and banging of blocks.

"Here—lay hold an' pull with me," Seth yelled in his ear. As they tugged on the rope, the foretopsail yard swung slowly to catch the wind, and the ship gathered way once more.

"Now the main brace," shouted Seth, darting aft. As Rod turned to run after him in the dark, he tripped over a coil of rope and would have sprawled flat if a huge hand had not caught him by the arm.

"Easy thar, Sonny," came the deep bass chuckle above him, and he looked up at a mighty figure silhouetted against the sails. It was the biggest man he had ever seen, coal black, with white teeth flashing in a grin.

"Bes' look whar you goin'," the rumbling voice continued, "or you be sha'k bait 'fo' you knows it."

"Thanks!" Rod managed to say as he hurried to join Seth at the rope.

When the canvas was close-hauled and the ship was reaching to the southeast with the wind abeam, the boys went forward to the lee of the forecastle hatch.

"Who was that who grabbed me when I fell over the rope?" Rod asked. "Did you see him? He looked as big as a barn door."

"I didn't see what happened," Seth laughed, "but it must have been the harpooner—the one they call Lucifer. He don't have much truck with the crew, but I've seen him prowling 'round the deck—at night, mostly. I know what you mean. Scares you the first time you get a look at him. He's so powerful I reckon he could bash in a whaleboat with his fist. But he never harms anything—only sparm whales."

IV

IT WAS daylight when all hands were called on
deck. A cold, steel-gray sea, flecked with windy
white, rolled to the gray horizon. As Seth foretold,
they had left the dunes of Nantucket somewhere
astern during the night.

There was breakfast—warmed-over chowder,
hardtack and some black, harsh-tasting stuff the
cook called coffee. As soon as they had eaten, men
from both watches were set to holystoning the deck.
As far as Rod could see, the planking was spotless
before they started, but that made no difference to

Mike Flynn. He drove them constantly, cursing the clumsy men, flicking the lazy ones with the end of a knotted rope.

It was hard work, but Rod had expected that. Years of farming and fishing had toughened him and he stuck at it till the last inch of deck gleamed white.

About noon the wind backed around to the north of west, and the yards had to be squared once more. Captain Beale, pacing the quarterdeck, looked aloft and ordered more canvas laid on. "We'll make the best of our easting while we can," Rod heard him tell the first mate.

A moment later the boy found himself clinging to the main topgallant yard, seventy feet above the deck. Getting up there had been easy enough, but trying to shake out the huge sail while he balanced on the swaying foot-rope was another matter. Out beyond him, toward the tip of the yard, Seth grinned encouragingly.

"You're lucky!" he yelled. "First time I went aloft 'twas at night, in a nor'east gale. Let go the clew lines. That's it! There she goes!"

They made their way down the ratlines once more, and went forward to the bows.

"I told you Beale was a lucky skipper," said the New Bedford boy, perching himself on a coil of tarry cable. "Look at this wind—fair astern. What every whaler hopes for is a chance to ride the wester-lies down to the Azores or Cape Verde. There's a few whales around there. Then, once we're through the horse latitudes—around thirty degrees north—we'll pick up the northeast trades an' head for the coast o' Brazil. Getting out o' the doldrums along the equator is generally quite a chore, but after that we can make a reach of it across the southeast trades, most o' the way to the Horn."

Rod was impressed. "Gosh," he said, "you sound 'most as if you could navigate it yourself!"

"I will, some day," the younger lad replied with confidence. "I can work a sextant right now—my dad showed me. After this voyage I'll be old enough to handle a mate's berth. There've been plenty o' New Bedford an' Nantucket whalemen that captained ships before they were twenty-five."

Rod, looking off over the port bow, suddenly jerked his arm up. "Look!" he cried. "Isn't that a—a whale?"

Less than a quarter of a mile to leeward he had seen a misty column rise from the sea and blow away on the wind. There was nobody aloft at the mastheads, but a lookout in the fore shrouds now sang out.

"Blo-o-ows!" came the call. "Three points on the la'board bow! Thar she breaches—finback!"

Rod was wide-eyed with excitement, but to his surprise there was no feverish activity aboard the *Pelican*. Mr. Macomber came forward and stood near them, his hands in his pockets. Meanwhile the whale swam calmly forward on a course that looked as if it would converge with their own. Every few seconds a huge gray fin like that of a shark would break water and they could see the long curve of the monster's back.

"He's playing—just like a porpoise," Seth remarked. "They'll do that. Sometimes keep a ship company for half a day."

"But aren't we going to lower?" Rod asked.

"Shucks, no. There isn't enough blubber on a finback to pay for the work. An' he's too fast to catch with a boat. See how he's built—long an' slim?"

They had a fine view of the whale now, for it was only some fifty yards away. Just as the New Hampshire boy was sure there would be a collision, the finback sheered off, flirted its great flukes in the air and departed for the ocean depths.

To Rod's unpracticed eye the whale had looked nearly as long as the ship.

"Wasn't that a big one?" he asked.

" 'Bout average," said Seth. "Maybe seventy-five feet. They're so common offshore here we don't pay much attention to 'em. No real sparm whaler would waste a harpoon on a finback."

* * *

For five more days the breeze held and the *Pelican* forged southwestward at a steady clip. Then there came a morning when the air had a warm and lazy feel to it, far different from the bitter winter winds that had brought them from New England. The sea was calm and blue, with patches of purple and emerald.

"M-m-m!" breathed Seth, drawing a deep lungful of air and unbuttoning his jacket. "We're in the Gulf Stream. You can 'most smell the tropics!"

Rod stowed his boots and reefer below, and came on deck in shirt and dungarees. There was plenty of work to be done, for the captain ordered more sail set in the light air. Rod went up the ratlines, past the topsails and topgallantsails—up and up to the dizzy heights of the main royal yard. He was getting the hang of it now, and the swaying of the spars no longer frightened him. Scrambling out along the stirrup rope he let go the sail as smartly, he flattered himself, as any first-class topman.

Just over his head, as he returned to the crosstrees, he saw Asa Tetlow, the cooper, lashing a pair of iron hoops to the slim mast above the royal yard. And the boy's heart beat faster, for he knew that this was the masthead lookout. From now on keen eyes would be on the watch for whales.

Hardly had he returned to the deck when Flynn bawled out an order for all hands to come aft.

"All you that have sailed in this ship before stand by yer reg'lar boats," he shouted. "Farmers, wharf-rats an' jimmy-ducks, line up here fer choosin'."

Rod supposed he came under the latter classification, so he joined the straggling ranks of the new-comers. At once the captain and the four mates began picking oarsmen by turn.

Seth, rated as an old hand, was already standing in the group before Injun John's boat. Somewhat to Rod's disappointment he was passed over when the third mate made his choice. But on the next round, Ezra Macomber pointed at him.

"This lad looks like he could pull an oar," the chief mate remarked. "Anyhow, we'll find out."

When all the foremast hands had been assigned their places, the New Hampshire boy found that the choosing had been done with some system. There were two greenhorns for each boat, teamed up with three more experienced oarsmen. The mate and boat-steerer completed the seven-man crew.

Rod had his first good look at Smiling Jimmy, the tall Kanaka, who stood at Macomber's side. He was a powerfully built fellow, dressed in nothing but short canvas pants. The muscles rippled under his satiny brown skin. He had a strong, high-cheek-boned face and his lips, drawn back in an easy grin, showed a row of splendid white teeth.

The rest of the boat's crew included two Portuguese—one of them the broad-backed Manuel—a Nantucketer named Ben Locker, Fred Girty, a pimply, mean-faced youth from the Boston wharves, and Rod, himself.

"All right, men, lower away," Captain Beale ordered. "We'll have our first boat practice right now. My crew'll stay aboard to work the ship."

It was an ideal morning for trying out the boats—a day of light air and smooth, easy swells. Lashings were cast off and the men piled into the four whaleboats, letting themselves down by the tackle from the davits.

Macomber stood in the stern, wielding a long steering oar, and Smiling Jimmy took his place in the bow. The others were motioned to the five rowing thwarts. Locker had the stroke oar, Rod was next, then the smaller Portuguese, then Girty, and Manuel pulled the bow oar.

The boat itself, something over twenty feet long, was a lightly built, double-ended affair that seemed to contain a surprising amount of gear for so small a craft. There was a centerboard well amidships, a mast and furled sail lying lengthwise across the thwarts, two big tubs of two-thirds-inch manila whale line, bailing buckets, a water keg, axes, knives, three harpoons and a couple of long, keen lances.

They got their oars in the water and fended off from the ship's side.

"All right, boys," said Macomber, "give way, now, an' spring to it lively."

Rod found the fourteen-foot ash blade a different matter from the oars he had used in his dory back home. Nevertheless, he watched Ben Locker's back and was soon pulling evenly, in rhythm with the stroke oar. Up forward, Girty seemed to be having trouble. The boat lurched as the Boston lad caught a crab, and there was some fluent Portuguese cursing from Manuel.

"Take hold o' that oar an' get your blade in square," Macomber admonished. "Now lay for'ard with the rest. Now back—way back, an' put some beef in it!"

The boat spurted ahead as the oars got into some kind of unison. They rowed with a will, urged on by the mate, and soon Rod saw that they had passed two of the other boats and were abreast of Flynn's crew.

"Come on, ye spalpeens—beat those lousy so-an'-

so's!" roared the second mate. But Macomber kept calm.

"Never mind a race, boys," he told them. "You've shown you can pull—that's all I wanted. Now step the mast an' let's try a bit o' sailing."

Manuel lifted the spar and thrust its foot through the hole in the forward thwart. The boom came down and the triangular sail shook out to catch what breeze there was.

"Drop the centerboard," Macomber called, and Rod, who was nearest, pulled the pin that held it up. Meanwhile the mate laid his big oar inboard and attached the sailing rudder to the stern-post. Ben Locker hauled the sheet and they skimmed along at a surprising pace, considering the light wind.

Rod felt more at home than he had at any time since he joined the *Pelican*. Small-boat sailing was right in his line. They ran before the wind for some ten minutes before the order was given to come about. As they tacked back toward the ship, Rod glanced at the sail and ventured a remark.

"She could take it a little closer to the wind," he suggested to Locker.

"All right, Jimmy-duck," the Nantucketer grinned. "She's all yours." And he shoved the sheet rope into the boy's hand.

Red-faced, Rod watched the edge of the sail as he hauled the boom an inch or two closer. He had been right. The light craft pointed higher and even gained a little speed.

"Laugh's on you, Ben," said Macomber. "The lad knows what he's doing. Take that sheet now, an' see if you can make out as well."

Locker accepted the rebuke with a scowl, but he was careful to keep the canvas drawing properly after that. As they came within hailing distance of the *Pelican,* the mate ordered the mast lowered and the oars out. They came up to the side with a flourish, the first boat back.

"Smartly, now," said Macomber. "Hook on to that tackle and up with her."

The captain was leaning on the rail when they climbed on deck.

"Looks like a pretty fair crew, Ezra," he commented. "Only saw you catch a crab once. Can't do that when you're going in on a whale, though. Better keep 'em at it every chance you get."

Forward by the forecastle hatch, out of hearing of the officers, Locker seized Rod's arm in powerful fingers.

"Kids that ain't dry behind the ears shouldn't try givin' advice to their betters," he growled.

Before he could say more the deep, soft voice of the Kanaka interrupted.

"Him-fella all right," said Smiling Jimmy. "You leave-um 'lone." Gently he took Locker's wrist and loosened his grip on Rod's arm. "You come 'long me, boy," he grinned. "We talky-talky."

Quite evidently Locker wanted no quarrel with the big brown South Sea Islander. As he slunk away, Smiling Jimmy led Rod forward and squatted on his heels in the lee of the capstan.

"You-fella, you all same good boatman," he told the boy. "Bimeby help catch-um plenty whale."

Rod thanked him and ventured a question. "Is it true you come from the Sandwich Islands?" he asked.

The Kanaka's face lighted up. "Hawaii," he said, rolling the musical word lovingly on his tongue. "Me come from Kona Coast of Big Islan'. Bes' canoemen in whole ocean live there."

In his pidgin English he went on to tell about his boyhood on the reefs at Kailua where the kings had their summer playground. He told of the prowess of Kamehameha's warriors, and how they had sailed in their great war canoes to conquer all the islands. And he told of the feasting at *luaus* in the palace grounds.

"Bimeby," he grinned, "maybe you-fella, you go Hawaii, eat plenty *poi*. You grow big an' strong all same Kanaka man."

"Gosh," said Rod, "I'd sure like to. Lagoons an'

palm trees, an' never any winter weather. It sounds 'most too good to be true."

"Plenty good," the brown man nodded. "But plenty bad things there too."

He described the flaming death that came from the great mountain, Mauna Loa, wiping out whole villages with its flow of molten lava. He told about hurricane winds that lashed high over the reefs and tore the grass roofs from the houses. And finally he mentioned the grisly habits of head-hunters.

"Missionary make-um big stone church at Kailua," he said. "Me-fella, me Christian. But back in hills, plenty Kanaka eat fella him kill. Keep head, dry-um, hang-um front of house."

Rod listened soberly. "I guess there are a few tough customers anywhere you go," he said. "But that won't keep me away from your islands, Jimmy, if I ever get the chance to see 'em."

A puff of wind from the northwest whipped the canvas taut, and the ship heeled to starboard. Clouds were forming on the horizon astern.

"Breeze is freshening," they heard Macomber shout to the third mate. "Better call the cap'n, an' send some men aloft to take in the royals. We're carrying a bit too much sail if it comes on to blow."

V

THE SHIP held her course steadily for a week, driving along under topsails on a booming northwest wind. Constant hard work and the hawk-eyed supervision of the mates had welded the crew into a fairly efficient unit. There was no more sea-sickness. Even the lubbers hustled on deck at the change of the watch, and only two or three were still too clumsy to reef or furl aloft.

Now that he had his sea legs, Rod bent all his energies to becoming a real sailor. He had thought he was strong and quick when he came aboard, but the

climbing and hauling had toughened his muscles and
put thick calluses on his hands. He endured the
labor and the stuffy sleeping quarters without com-
plaint. This was what he had gone to sea for. Even
the unvaried diet of jerked beef and flinty biscuit
wasn't too bad after he got used to chewing it.

There came a morning when the wind died suddenly and the ship rolled with fluttering sails. The
sea around them had an oily look and there were
patches of weed floating on the long swells.

"Reckon we're in the horse latitudes," Seth explained. "Never can tell whether we'll get a calm
or a blow in this part o' the Atlantic. An' the wind
can come from any place on the compass."

They were standing far up in the bows. Suddenly
Seth pointed off to starboard. "Flying fish!" he exclaimed. "Look! A whole school of 'em—an' something's after 'em."

The surface of the sea was broken by a glittering
swarm of small, bright-colored fish that skipped over
the water or sailed for many yards on their wing-
like fins.

Tedeconk, the Indian harpooner, had joined the
boys, moving on silent feet.

"Big fish chasing 'em,' he muttered. "Maybe
swordfish."

He departed as suddenly as he had appeared. In a minute or two he was back with a harpoon and a length of line in his hand. Letting himself down into the forechains he made one end of the line fast and hung by one hand, the shaft of the harpoon poised in the other.

The flying fish were all about the ship now. One of them made a terrified leap and skittered across the deck, bringing up against the bulwark. Seth grabbed for it. The next moment he held up his prize proudly. It was a fragile thing, less than half a pound in weight, tinted a lovely, iridescent blue. But before the boys had time to admire the fish, they heard a savage yell from the forechains.

Tedeconk was waving the wooden shaft in triumph. His iron, attached to the stout whale line, was deep in the side of a hundred-pound marlin that churned the water to white foam under the bows. The boys scrambled over the bulwark and helped the Indian haul the big fish in. Stretched out on the deck it was eight feet long, from the tip of its spike-like bill to its forked tail.

Two more swordfish were harpooned by the Gay Header before the flurry was over, and for a day the *Pelican's* crew reveled in fresh food. The cook served broiled swordfish steaks in the cabin, while the foremast hands had to be satisfied with chunks of the brownish meat boiled in the stew-pot. Even so, it was a welcome change from "salt-horse."

There was plenty of work for all hands during the week that followed. Light, changeable winds kept them setting and furling sail and hauling on the braces. Twice, when they found themselves completely becalmed, the captain ordered the boats lowered and they were given more practice at the oars.

Finally there came an evening when the breeze blew steadily out of the northeast. They set more sail, hauled the yards and set their course to the southeastward with the wind abeam. Three days later there were flocks of small, dark birds darting over the sea.

"That means land," Seth told Rod. "We're within a day's sailing o' the Cape Verdes, or I miss my guess. Those birds are Mother Carey's chickens."

The masthead lookout sighted land shortly after daybreak next morning, and within an hour the outline of purple mountains on the horizon could be seen from the deck. The Portuguese sailors grinned and gabbled in their native tongue, pointing excitedly toward the hilly island. Most of them had come originally from the Cape Verdes or the Azores.

Early that afternoon, the ship dropped anchor in the bay. The white buildings of a little town could

be seen, lining narrow streets that climbed steeply
from the shore.

Captain Beale picked a boat crew and sent them
ashore under the command of Sanchez, the third
mate. The only other Portuguese allowed to go was
Manuel, an old and trusted hand. The rest scowled
and cursed but had to content themselves with watching the boat pull toward the wharves.

It was close to sundown before the shore party
returned, the boat loaded almost to the gunwales
with provisions. When she came alongside, the crew
passed up bunches of bananas, bags of onions and
cabbages, a dozen plucked chickens and a live pig,
squealing and kicking.

Old "Chips," the ship's carpenter, must have had
warning of the pig's arrival, for he had thrown
together a stout pen, just forward of the try-works.

As soon as the cargo was brought aboard and the
boat hoisted to the davits, Captain Beale gave orders
to weigh anchor. By the time darkness fell, they were
out of the bay and clear of the reefs, heading southwesterly before the wind.

*   *   *

"Lookouts aloft!" ordered the first mate as the
sky began to lighten on the starboard quarter. "We're
on sperm whale ground an' the sun'll be up in another

quarter of an hour. Take the main-top, Jimmy. An' you, Glenn, skip up to the fore. Let's see how good your eyes are."

The big Kanaka didn't seem to move fast, but he beat Rod to the masthead in spite of Rod's eagerness. It was the first lookout the boy had been called to stand. He clambered up past the royal crosstrees and mounted the tiny platform on the skysail yard.

He seemed very far above the deck where the ant-like figures of seamen went about their morning duties. The ship was running under royals, and the wind made soft thunder in the canvas below him. The horizon ahead was still shrouded in darkness but he could look off across miles of whitecapped sea. He shivered a little in the dawn chill and grasped the iron hoops that railed the lookout.

After a little while he felt a glow of warmth on his back. He turned and saw the sun had climbed out of the sea. A wave to Smiling Jimmy brought an answering gesture of encouragement.

Rod swung back to the arc of ocean for which the mate had made him responsible. It was a full-time job, he realized, scanning those endless leagues of blue. And except for forecastle talk he didn't know exactly what he was looking for. He had heard some of the old hands arguing as to whether whales blew out water or steam, and they had described the sperm whale's spout as being low and rounded, "like a haystack." The right whale, on the other hand, shot a high stream that had a forward pitch to it.

He tried dividing the expanse of sea into segments and searching one after another. Then he remembered that a whale's spout might last only a few seconds, and that he was likely to miss it if he concentrated on only one area at a time.

For what seemed like hours he stood there on his swaying pinnacle, his eyes sweeping back and forth across the empty blue. It had a hypnotic effect on him. He felt himself growing drowsy and shook himself angrily to stay awake.

Then, out of the corner of his eye, he glimpsed a tiny spot of white that looked softer—and lasted longer—than the crest of a breaking wave. Two or three seconds passed and it was still there, a bushy little cloud, a good mile to leeward.

His lips trembled as he tried to form a word. At last it burst from his throat in a yell that had all his lung power behind it.

"Blows! Ah—blo-o-ows!"

The hail came back instantly from the deck. "Where away? Are ye sure it's sparm?"

Rod pointed with his outstretched arm. "A mile off on the port bow," he shouted. "What do you say it is, Jimmy?"

"Sparm whale!" the Kanaka answered. "Ah, blows!"

Below all was in an uproar. "Turn out all hands to lower!" the captain bellowed, as the two lookouts left their perches. Rod saw Smiling Jimmy grab a stay and slide from the crosstrees all the way to the deck. He attempted the same maneuver but scorched his hands after eight or ten feet and let himself down more slowly. The first mate's crew was already scrambling into the boat when he got there. He tumbled over the gunwale and found his place while the mate and the harpooner let down the falls. As it was, they were the last boat to hit the water.

"Fend off, there!" yelled Macomber. "Now—all oars together. Give way! Spring to it, ye tigers! Pull —pull—pull!"

As he gave them the beat, they whipped their oars through the water and shot away from the ship, close in the wake of Flynn's boat. Rod had never worked as hard in his life as he did in the next ten minutes. It was backbreaking, breathless rowing, but in the excitement of the chase he felt no exhaustion.

All four boats were nearly abreast and only a quarter of a mile from the whale when there was a cry from the men in the bows.

"There go flukes! He's sounded!"

"Ease off, men," said the mate. "He'll be down a spell—maybe an hour. We don't want to run too far past him."

The other boats drifted, spread out over three or four hundred yards of sea. Panting, the crews leaned on their oars.

"Well, Glenn," Macomber grinned, "you did a good job, your first trick at the masthead. There's a bounty comin' to you—ten pounds o' 'baccy for the first whale sighted."

"Haw!" jeered Ben Locker. "What good'll it do him? The young lubber don't even chaw!"

He shifted his own cud from left cheek to right and spat expertly to leeward.

Rod flushed. "Tell you what I'll do," he answered. "I'll trade the tobacco for that sheath knife you're wearing."

Macomber looked pleased. "It's a fair swap, Ben," he told the Nantucketer. "You got a spare knife, an' ten pounds o' prime blackjack's a good price."

It was Locker's turn to do some squirming. He thought it over a moment and then swung around on the thwart. "It's a deal," he said sullenly. "Soon's ye git the 'baccy, I'll trade ye the knife."

They had a rest of close to half an hour, watching the sea ahead and on both sides for the whale's reappearance. Suddenly there was a hoarse whisper from Macomber.

"Thar he breaches! Right astern! Quiet now—pull her 'round with the port oars. Ready with the first iron, Jimmy!"

Looking past the mate while he pulled, Rod saw a huge, black, squarish mass subsiding into the water behind them. In a moment the boat was turned and headed toward the blind forehead of the whale. The boy could no longer see what was happening in the bow but he caught a glimpse of the second mate's boat closing in fast.

"Sta'board oars—steady now—we're on the eye!" Macomber whispered. Then, with a yell, "Let him have it, Jimmy!"

There was a quiver in the hull as the big Kanaka hurled his iron.

"We're fast!" shouted the mate. "Back water, now. Lively—out o' reach of his flukes!"

At the same moment he pulled the steering oar in and sprang forward over the thwarts to change places with the boat-steerer. As soon as the Kanaka reached the stern he passed a turn of whale line over the loggerhead and seized the long oar.

Rod had a good view of the whale now. Its monstrous bulk was partly out of water and he could see where the harpoon had gone into its side clear to the hitches. At that instant the enormous flukes of the tail rose thirty feet out of the sea and descended with a thunderous crash. The boat, half filled with water, rolled so far over that Rod thought he would be tossed into the sea.

By a miracle she righted herself, just as the whale plunged beneath the surface.

"Keep clear o' that line!" roared Macomber. The tough manila was spinning out of the first tub, making the bend around the loggerhead and whipping forward past the oarsmen on its way to the bow chocks. As the sounding whale gathered speed the boat was jerked around, end for end.

"He's makin' his run!" shouted the mate. "Ship oars an' start bailin'."

Rod seized the leather bucket under the thwart and began throwing water over the side as fast as he could. They were speeding through the waves at race-horse speed now, the other boats left far behind. High in the stern stood the Kanaka boat-steerer, swinging easily on his oar and grinning with delight. This, obviously, was what he loved. Speed and danger and matching his skill against terrible odds. Rod, who had been scared almost out of his wits at first, felt his own courage coming back as he watched Smiling Jimmy.

They were well into the second tub of line before

the weary whale returned to the surface. It came up sluggishly, without breaching, and they saw its bushy spout only a hundred yards ahead.

"Oars!" Macomber snapped. "You, Manuel, start haulin' line. Bring me in right aft o' the hump, Jimmy."

Rod felt the mounting tension as they pulled cautiously nearer. He knew a sperm whale's eye was low on the side of its head and it could only see objects directly abeam. The Kanaka was coming in on the big beast's quarter, far enough back to be out of sight.

Up in the bow the mate stood ready, knee firmly planted in the notched cleat, lance poised to strike. Suddenly, when they were a dozen feet from its side, the whale gave a convulsive movement. Something had made it uneasy. With all his strength, Macomber darted the long lance deep into the side below the hump.

"Starn all!" he yelled. "Starn—for your lives!"

All together the oars bit the water and the boat sprang back from its quarry. The action was none too quick, for the whale gave a stroke with its flukes that drove its whole vast body upward and forward in a terrifying leap. If they had been lying side-to, the wave it made would surely have swamped them.

As it was, such a cascade of water came over the bow that the boat was filled nearly to the thwarts.

Frantically bailing, Rod heard a yell of triumph from the mate.

"Got his vitals!" Macomber cried. "He spouts red! Starn all, now, an' look out for the flurry!"

Again they seized the oars and put another score of yards between themselves and the wounded monster. It thrashed aimlessly for a few seconds, then breached. Rod held his breath, for the shadow of that awful body lay over the boat. He saw the huge, blunt head—the twenty-foot jaw hanging open —the rows of terrible teeth. As it fell back into the sea and the waves subsided, there was a tinge of crimson in the green water.

"All right, boys," said the mate calmly. "That does it. Haul in your line an' coil it down."

VI

DURING the excitement of the battle, Rod had lost all track of time. Looking up at the sun now, he was surprised to realize that it was still morning. The whole chase had taken less than two hours.

When they lifted on a wave crest they could see one or two of the other boats in the distance. The *Pelican* was hull-down over the horizon, but from the slant of her sails it was evident that she was making all speed to come up with them.

For half an hour the men were kept busy recovering whale line. Their catch had taken some two

hundred and fifty fathoms out of the tubs in its
rush to escape. Now it had to be hauled in and coiled
with the utmost care, so that it would run out
smoothly the next time it was used.

Ezra Macomber lolled in the stern-sheets and
viewed their prize with satisfaction.

"Ought to make mighty close to a hundred barrels," he said. "A good fat bull—not the biggest I
ever saw, but plenty o' blubber."

The immense bulk of the dead whale wallowed
in the trough of the waves. Sharks had gathered,
drawn by the stain of blood in the sea, and their
sharp, triangular fins moved around the drifting
boat in slow circles. Rod was watching one of them
when it made a sudden rush for the whale's side. He
saw the cruel jaws open as the shark rolled belly-up,
and a two-foot gash appeared in the shiny black
skin. An involuntary shudder went through the boy.
It was his first sight of a big shark at close range and
it gave him a horror of the beasts that was to last a
long time.

Within half an hour the second mate's boat came
up to them, and ten minutes later the *Pelican* swung
into the wind a few hundred yards away. The two
boats towed the carcass of the whale alongside and
it was made fast to the ship by a cable passed around
the "small" of the tail, just ahead of the flukes.

The other boats had already been taken aboard. Standing in the waist, the skipper looked down at the catch and grinned.

"Good work, Mr. Macomber," he said. "Get your men aboard, and give them some breakfast. Soon as they've eaten we'll start cutting in."

Rod was hungrier than he had realized. He ate his jerky and biscuit, washed them down with a drink of tepid water from the scuttlebutt, and hurried to the rail to watch the rigging of the cutting-stage. A couple of heavy planks were run out over the whale, the inboard ends suspended by ropes let down over the side, and the outer extremities held by tackles from the mainmast. A third plank, nearly thirty feet long, was bolted across the ends of the first two, and a light handrail gave the men working on the outer stage some measure of security.

Seth joined Rod at the rail. "We'll all have plenty o' work when the blubber starts coming aboard," he said. "Quite a start you made, for your first voyage. Some o' the crew say you've brought the ship luck."

Ezra Macomber came from the cabin companion with a bulky package in his hand.

"Glenn," he called. "Glenn and Locker."

Ben Locker shambled aft with Rod, and the first mate held up the bundle of tobacco. "Here you are, lad," he said. "Hand over the knife and sheath, Ben."

Locker unbuckled the knife from his belt and passed it to Rod with a grin. Then he took the tobacco.

"Reckon I got the best o' that trade," he jeered. "I'm fixed fer chawin' fer a year. Still, long as you don't use the stuff, I guess we're both well off."

Rod drew the blade from the sheath and admired its keen edge. It was a good knife, well-balanced and of true Sheffield steel. He fastened the leather sheath at his side and congratulated himself on a profitable day's work.

Flynn and Injun John went out on the cutting-stage, armed with sharp-edged blubber spades and began driving deep gashes just back of the monstrous head. A tackle was made fast to the jaw and the whale's body was slowly revolved, while the two mates completed their cutting all around the "neck."

Meanwhile the crew was rigging a pair of huge falls from the main top. The blocks were as big as barrels, and rove through them were three-inch cables, with their running ends fast to the drum of a windlass.

From the lower block of each fall hung an immense iron hook—a blubber hook, as Seth explained to Rod. Just back of the partly severed head, Flynn was now dexterously slicing a lengthwise slit. After four or five feet, he changed direction and brought his cut down the whale's side toward the ship. Next, with a quick jab or two, he made a hole near the top and yelled for the tackle. As the block creaked down he thrust the hook through the hole and stood back.

"Haul, ye spalpeens!" he roared.

A dozen hands began heaving on the windlass. For a moment the ropes strained taut and nothing seemed to happen. Then the great strip of blubber came away with a tearing sound, and peeled neatly off as the whale's body rolled.

As the end of the blanket strip rose, the two mates worked furiously with their spades, keeping the cut even. The weight of the huge mass of blubber had heeled the ship over at an angle, and oil, dripping on the deck, made the footing slippery.

"Vast heaving!" bellowed Flynn. The strip had been hauled as far as it would go toward the main truck, and they held it there while Injun John cut another hole, thirty feet below the first. The second tackle was run down and the blubber hook inserted. With a long-handled boarding sword, Flynn slashed through the strip above the hook, and the first blanket piece swung heavily inboard, knocking the unwary Fred Girty into the scuppers.

Manuel opened the main hatch, just forward of

the try-works, and the blanket was let down into
the blubber room. Meanwhile the men at the windlass started heaving again and the blubber continued
to unwind off the whale's carcass, much as a house-
wife peels an apple.

"Glenn!" shouted the first mate. "Get below with
Manuel and cut up that blubber."

Barefooted, and wearing only his rolled-up
dungarees, Rod jumped down into the greasy mass.
Manuel handed him a big blubber-knife.

"Look," he told him. "Like dees." And the
Portuguese proceeded to slice off a chunk and toss it
to the other side of the blubber room. Rod had
heard enough about the operation to know these
sections were known as "horse-pieces." Clumsily at
first, but gaining skill as he went on, he followed
Manuel's example.

It was a dirty business, for the whole cramped
space was saturated with oil, and the boy was
constantly slipping and falling. Blubber, he discovered, was not mere fat. It was a tough, fine-
grained substance that looked like lean beef. To his
surprise it had no unpleasant smell.

The horse-pieces were chopped up by men with
mincing knives and thrown into a hopper ready to be
fed to the try-pots. A fire had been built on the brick
hearth under the giant kettles, and after the first boil-

ing there was no lack of fuel. Crisp scraps of refuse blubber, from which the oil had been tried, gave a hot, steady flame.

Rod was ordered back on deck after two hours of backbreaking work. From head to foot he dripped blood and oil, but there was no time to clean up now. Glad to be up in the fresh air, he pitched in with the windlass crew and the frantic labor went on, uninterrupted. This was a big whale, and there would be no rest for anybody aboard the *Pelican* till the job was finished, even though it took all day and all night.

At midafternoon, the cook came around with a big can of muddy coffee which they gulped down while they worked. By that time the blubber had been stripped off almost to the "small."

The Kanaka harpooner had now relieved Flynn on the cutting-stage and he and Injun John turned their attention to the head once more. Cutting it off was a task for real craftsmen. They had to chop through nearly twenty feet of blubber, bone and sinew and finally through the great backbone itself.

At the end of a half hour of furious work, Smiling Jimmy gave a yell of triumph. The head tore loose with a mighty splash and swung astern, held only by the chain around the jaw. The final strip of blubber was hauled up and the cable around the tail was cast off. Rolling in the seas, the huge carcass drifted out from the ship's side. Instantly, the sharks, which had been hanging about for hours, charged in to worry the great, bloody mass. And from the air came broad-winged frigate birds and albatrosses, sailing upwind to perch on the body and gorge themselves.

Ever since midday two men had been working over the try-pots, feeding minced blubber in from the port side and dipping out the clean, hot oil into a big cooling tank to starboard. As soon as it had cooled sufficiently, it was bailed out into huge casks that held 350 gallons each. Asa Tetlow, the cooper, headed the casks and tightened the iron hoops, pounding away constantly with his hammer.

Wrestling the filled casks out of the way was a difficult and dangerous job on the rolling, slippery deck. No greenhorns were allowed to tackle it, for one clumsy move might overturn the great barrel and crush its handlers against the bulwarks.

To Rod, the most fascinating part of the whole cutting-in process came next. It was nearly sunset when they hauled the whale's head back to the stage. Injun John chopped two holes at the sides of the vast, flat forehead, and both blubber-hooks were attached. Then, with a great straining and heaving at the windlass, the whole thirty-ton mass was hoisted two-thirds of the way out of water.

With a monkey rope about his waist, Smiling Jimmy clambered to the top of the head and made an exploratory jab or two with the spade. When he was sure he had the right spot, he cut straight down into the "case"—the deep reservoir of pure spermaceti that made the sperm whale the richest catch in the sea.

Through the two-foot opening he prepared, a big bucket was dropped from the overhead tackle and brought up brimming with clear, white, sweet-smelling liquid. No trying out was needed for the contents of the case. It was dumped into clean casks immediately. And before the well was empty they took nearly 2000 gallons of the precious stuff from the whale's head.

All that evening and far on into the night the crew worked like demons in the red glow of the try-works fires. They munched salt-horse and biscuit, flavored with the oil that dripped from their hands, swigged a hasty drink from the water butt and went back to their jobs.

Rod thought he had never been so tired in all his life. More than once he nearly went to sleep on his feet. But the snarling commands of Flynn and the occasional flick of a rope's end would bring him back to consciousness and start him heaving on the windlass once more.

It was past two in the morning when the last cask was under hatches and the tackle lowered and stowed.

"Get to your bunks, men," said Captain Beale wearily. "We'll keep her hove-to the rest o' the night. You've done well today. That whale made an even hundred barrels."

Like one in a trance, Rod stumbled down the ladder and into his bunk, barely remembering to strip off his greasy trousers. He was asleep almost before he hit the straw tick, and there he lay like a log till morning.

At eight o'clock all hands were routed out to clean ship. The weather and wind held fair, and the *Pelican's* sails were set to continue her southwesterly passage. Meanwhile every inch of deck and gear had to be scrubbed and washed down and scrubbed again.

"Hope we don't sight another whale today," Seth grinned. "I've seen it happen, though—start dirtying the decks five minutes after the last job o' cleaning was done."

"Are we still in whale waters?" asked Rod. "I'd sure like to have the fun of raising another spout from the masthead."

"We might get another," Seth nodded. "We're

pretty well past the Western Island Grounds, but we might catch up with a traveler, heading for the South Seas just like we are."

But as matters turned out, it was many a day before Rod had a chance to sight another whale.

That night the breeze grew stronger, to the point where royals and topgallantsails had to be taken in. For three days they boomed along under topsails with half a gale pushing them on. Then came a lull followed by thunder squalls. And on the fifth morning after the cutting in, the port watch came on deck to find the sea glassy calm.

As the sun rose higher, it beat down mercilessly on the idle ship. Rod laid a careless hand on the metal of the capstan and snatched it away as if he had touched a hot stove. Even the deck planking blistered his bare feet.

Seth, looking over the side, pointed to a patch of yellowish weed.

"Reckon we'll just have to sweat it out for a spell," he said with a wry face. "I figured we must be getting down close to the Line, an' sure enough, here we are in the doldrums."

VII

THE WEEK that followed was a trying time for all on board. Each morning the sun sprang out of the sea with burning heat. No wind ruffled the oily surface. The ship rocked gently on the light swells and her sails hung limp.

Not even Flynn could find tasks to keep the crew occupied. The heat in the forecastle was stifling, so they lolled about on deck, keeping in the shade of the motionless sails. The only relief from the monotony was an occasional thunder shower that brought a brief torrent of warm rain, falling straight downward and leaving the deck steaming.

From constant exposure to the sun, Rod's body took on a deep coat of tan. He was almost as dark as Smiling Jimmy. Seth, with his fair skin, was less fortunate. He burned, peeled and freckled by turns.

While the rest of the crew drowsed, argued or told interminable stories, the two boys found their own diversion. Sometimes they dropped big hooks over the side and hauled up masses of weed, marveling over the strange sea creatures that lived in it.

There were minute shellfish; tiny squid, with bodies hardly bigger than a finger-end and thread-like, writhing tentacles; clusters of flying fish eggs, and dozens of other forms of life which they could not identify.

At other times they fished with handlines over the side. Their hooks were baited with small squid taken from the weed, but there were few fish to be found in those sluggish waters. The only catches they made were an occasional flying fish and a three-foot shark that had swallowed the tackle. In trying to recover his hook, Rod came near losing a hand, for even though he had been careful to kill the shark first, some reflex action brought its teeth together with a cruel snap when he started to reach inside its mouth.

So the time dragged by. Each day at noon the first mate took a sight on the sun and Rod stood as close as he dared, watching the operation. Once he heard Macomber give his report to the captain.

"Current's bearing south, right enough," the tall mate said. "Made around forty miles since yesterday."

It was hard to believe that they were drifting nearly two miles an hour but it must have been true. For on the eighth day, early in the afternoon, they ran into a southerly squall.

As soon as he saw the black clouds off the port bow, Captain Beale called all hands to shorten sail. The wind was violent when it came. Under reefed topsails, the *Pelican* reared and pitched like a bucking horse. But within half an hour the sudden storm had blown itself out, and they were cruising through clear, bright weather with a steady southeasterly breeze on their beam.

*   *   *

It was early April now. Spring would be coming at home, but south of the Line it was autumn, and the weather grew steadily cooler and the days shorter as they bowled along on their southeasterly course.

One night watch, when Rod and Seth stood together at the wheel, the New Bedford boy pointed to a bright group of stars, low on the horizon ahead.

"That's the Southern Cross," he said. "Now you've seen it you can call yourself a real shellback."

The South Atlantic was a lonely place. They had raised no land since leaving the Cape Verdes, and not once in all those weeks had they seen a ship. Then, one fine morning, there were three or four sails in sight at once.

"Look!" Rod called. "What are they, Seth? Whalers?"

The other boy ran up the rigging for a better view. "No," he said. "They look to me like clippers out o' Salem an' Baltimore—probably headed for California an' the gold fields. See how they're crowding canvas? That biggest one, to the north, must be logging eighteen knots. And every one of 'em's carrying skysails an' staysails!"

The hurrying merchantmen soon left the clumsy *Pelican* far astern, and she sailed once more through an empty sea. The lookouts stood all day at the mastheads with never a glimpse of a spout. When Rod took his turn aloft, he found it hard to keep awake. Searching those endless leagues of unbroken ocean had a hypnotic effect on him.

One afternoon, high on the fore royal yard, he shook himself out of a drowsy half stupor in time to see a row of sleek black backs breaking the water a mile or more ahead. At first he thought they were porpoises and said nothing. Then he realized that these were bigger than any porpoises he had ever seen.

"Hey—Manuel," he called to the man in the main-top. "What do you call those things out there? Are they whales?"

The Portuguese shaded his eyes with a brown hand.

"Blackfeesh!" he cried. "Ahoy dere, below! Blackfeesh off de bow!"

The call was greeted by a general uproar on deck. Rod heard the order to lower the boats and scuttled down the ratlines to get to his place. He had time to shoot a question at Seth as the other lad hurried past.

"What is a blackfish, anyway?" he asked.

"Sort of a small whale," Seth replied over his shoulder. "Second cousin to a sparm, I reckon."

The four boats hit the water almost together and the rowers bent to their oars, glad to get into action again. Within twenty minutes they were hauling up on the school, which had submerged briefly, then surfaced again close ahead of them. A final drive of the oars sent the first mate's boat right in among the dark, glistening backs.

Smiling Jimmy launched his first iron, then

whirled and put a second harpoon in another black-fish that lay close aboard. In an instant both animals dived, and the boat went tearing through the water, fouling lines and being followed by curses from the other crews.

Luckily the two harpooned blackfish chose to flee in the same direction. Ezra Macomber, who had scrambled forward as soon as the irons were fast and changed places with the Kanaka, crouched in the bow with ax in hand, ready to cut a line if necessary. But after a run of two or three hundred yards the wounded blackfish broke water once more and huddled close together as if for mutual protection. Hauling in fast, the boat was alongside in a moment. The mate lanced them both and they died with hardly a flurry.

In spite of the ease with which they had been captured, the size of the beasts was surprising to Rod. Each one measured nearly thirty feet in length and, except for a rounded forehead, they looked very much like miniature sperm whales.

The boat's crew had no help in towing their double catch back to the ship, for each of the other craft had killed one blackfish. It was a long, tough pull and nearly two hours passed before all five bodies were made fast along the *Pelican's* side. Through the rest of the day and all that night the hands were kept busy stripping blubber and trying it out. And by dawn they had added more than fifty barrels of fairly good oil to the cargo in the hold.

Around latitude 30 south, the ship ran out of the southeast trades and into more variable weather. For a month the men had had little work on the yards and braces. Now they had to scramble aloft a dozen times a day to set more sail in periods of calm, or take it in when sudden squalls appeared. One day the log might show a good gain; the next, they would roll in the long swells, practically becalmed.

After a week of it, the crew was glad to find steady winds once more. They were some four hundred miles off the River Plate when they picked up the Westerlies. The wind came in over the starboard beam, blowing strong and fresh with a bite of autumn in it. Holding her course southwestward, the *Pelican* ran close-hauled under topsails and staysails. For all her clumsy lines she pointed well into the wind, and day after day she logged better than a hundred sea miles.

Even at that speed it was another two weeks before they sighted the Falkland Islands. For twenty-four hours they had been running through trailing wisps of fog that obscured any view of the sea for more than a few cables' lengths ahead. Then, one cold morning when the port watch came on deck, the air cleared suddenly. On the sharp, blue line of the horizon, off the starboard bow, there was a low-lying smudge of gray.

Old "Chips," the carpenter, gave a chuckle at the sight and blew on his gnarled hands. "Yep," he said. "I was right. Thought I felt a chill in the air last night. Figgered we'd see land today. When ye raise the Falklands it's time to break out yer reef-coats an' heavy-weather clothes. Goin' to need 'em from here to the Horn."

They kept well to leeward of the islands, but by mid-morning they had a clear view of the rocky shore and the drab-looking moorland, climbing to desolate hills. Out of one of the bays came a white dot of sail. It was a British cutter, fore-and-aft rigged and skimming along under a huge mainsail and a bellying jib. She cut across their bows and gave them a hail. The skipper replied through his speaking trumpet.

"Whaler *Pelican,* Captain Beale, out o' New Bedford," he told the cutter. "Bound for the Pacific by way o' Cape Horn. Any news?"

"Not much," the British officer answered. "We spoke another whaler two days ago. *Abigail Slocum,* from Nantucket. You may overtake her."

Captain Beale thanked the cutter's commander and the graceful craft dipped her colors. Then she swept past their stern and started clawing back to harbor against the wind, her towering mast heeled far to starboard.

Rod had a blue moment as he watched her go. With land so near, he would have given almost anything for a day ashore, with the feel of springy turf under his feet.

Seth brought him back to reality with a poke in the ribs and a grin. "You're a sailor now," said the New Bedford boy. "Remember?"

The veteran Matty Gage was standing by the fore weather shrouds, a few feet away.

"So the *Abigail Slocum's* close ahead of us," he remarked. "Must ha' sailed right after we did. I used to know a feller aboard her. Worst ship he was ever in, he claimed. Her skipper's a mean, penny-pinchin' old cuss, an' he's got a couple o' bucko mates under him that never let up on the crew. Glad I ain't sailin' in her!"

Before that day was over they had proof of the truth of old Chips' prophecy. As the watches changed, the men came on deck bundled up in woolen clothes and slickers. Rod, wet with spray and shivering, went aft to the slop chest and drew a sou'-wester and oilskins against his future pay.

Each day as they bowled southward the air grew colder and the wind blew harder. Captain Beale

made no secret of the fact that he meant to drive his
ship to the limit, for he wanted to clear Cape Horn
before the late June storms. So they ran under topsails and courses and only shortened sail when the
gale threatened to carry away some of their canvas.

It was rough work aloft on the yards in such
weather. Once a sudden snow-squall caught them
while they were reefing topsails, and Rod, out at the
tip of the main topsail yard, found the canvas so stiff
with ice it was like clawing at a sheet of iron. He
clung there in the blast for ten minutes, until belaying pins were passed up to the yardarms. With one
of them he was able to club away the thickest of the
ice and get enough play in the sail to make fast his
reef points. When he came down his hands were so
scraped and sore he could hardly close them.

That was when he discovered that "the Doctor,"
as the ship's cook was always called, really deserved
his nickname. The old colored man was standing by
the galley door as Rod stumbled past.

"Here, son," he called. "Lemme see dem han's o'
yourn. Got somep'n here to fix 'em."

He held a pan of warm sperm oil, saved for just
such emergencies. At his bidding Rod plunged his
fists into the oil, then rubbed it over his skin. The
stuff was as soothing as any ointment.

For a week they hardly saw the sun. Then one day

at noon it appeared for a few moments between racing clouds. Rod was aft near the wheel, polishing the brasswork of the binnacle, when Mr. Macomber hurried on deck with his instruments.

"Quick, lad," he said. "Drop that rag and keep an eye on the chronometer. When it hits twelve o'clock, give me the word."

Rod watched the hands on the dial creep toward noon and shouted his signal when they marked the exact hour of twelve. The sun was beginning to edge behind a cloud, but the mate had his sextant in position and took a good sight.

Rod took courage from the tall man's look of satisfaction. "What do you make our latitude, sir?" he asked.

Macomber glanced at him in some surprise. "Near enough the fifty-eighth parallel south," he said. "I'll have to work it out to the minute on paper, but you'll see the helm put over as soon as I report to the cap'n."

Within a quarter of an hour that was just what happened. The order was passed to haul 'round on the yards, and the two men at the wheel brought the ship's head into the howling wind. With the green seas coming over her bows at every wave, she began fighting her way westward.

From that time on, the crew worked in a nightmare of swirling water. When they went forward or aft they had to cling desperately to hand-lines rigged the length of the ship's waist, and after each sea they battled hip-deep through an icy deluge.

Water seeped in around the hatches and cascaded down the companionways. Even in the forecastle, the chests and sea-bags were adrift, sloshing back and forth as the ship pitched and rolled. And for ninety hours not a man of them had a dry stitch on him.

At the end of each watch, Rod tumbled into his bunk as he was—wet, shivering and exhausted. Too tired to dream, he slept like a dead man till he was called to work again.

Much of the time, day and night, all hands were needed on deck, for it took the full strength of the crew to haul the yards when the ship was put about. The wind, already at gale force, seemed to grow even fiercer as they beat to westward. They had shortened down to a storm jib, double-reefed topsails on the fore and main and a spanker on the mizzen. It was stout, new canvas, yet on the second day the fore topsail split right down the middle with a sound like a cannon shot. Before a single man could scramble to the yard, the sail had ripped itself to ribbons.

In peril of their lives the best topmen in the crew

bent fresh canvas to the spar, and the *Pelican* labored on.

Rod had lost all track of time, but it must have been on the fourth day of beating to windward that the warning of disaster came.

The lookout perched in the crosstrees saw it first— a bank of inky black cloud rolling up at incredible speed on the western horizon. His frightened cry brought the officers on deck at a run.

"Call all hands!" yelled Captain Beale. "Get the sails furled—double gaskets—all but the spanker. You, Sails and Chips—rig a drogue we can ride to. Make it a big one—plenty o' cable. Inside o' ten minutes you'll see a blow like you've never seen before!"

Under the driving of Mike Flynn the men sprang to furious action. They swarmed out on the yards, clawed in the bucking topsails and held them with their bodies until stout lashings were passed around the tight-furled canvas. The jib was run down and stowed before it could whip free. Panting at the windlass, the men hauled two hundred fathoms of the heaviest cable up from the forehold and stretched it in great loops along the deck, while the sailmaker and carpenter worked like beavers to fashion a sea anchor out of crossed spars and canvas.

A sudden darkness made Rod look upward. The

wind-torn edge of the great black cloud was right over them now, and a gloom like that of night covered the heaving sea.

"All right, boys!" shouted the mate. "Hang on for your lives—here she comes!"

VIII

BLINDLY Rod staggered across to the fore shrouds and gripped them with both hands, bracing his feet against an iron bollard. There was a sound in the air—a high-pitched, soul-shaking sound like the howling of a million wolves. He had heard the scream of wind many times, but this was all the winds of heaven screaming with one voice.

The blast hit them with the force of a battering ram. It caught the ship a little to starboard of head-on and threw her almost on her beam ends. The naked masts were bent like saplings. One of the forestays parted with a crack like a pistol shot but the others held. Rod, hanging precariously from the shroud, saw that only the fore topgallant mast had carried away.

The ship was struggling like a wounded animal. At last she righted herself, but under the pounding of wind and water she was falling off into the trough of the waves.

"Get that drogue over!" yelled Macomber. The order was echoed by Flynn's bull-like roar and a dozen men raced forward to the improvised sea anchor. With a mighty heave they launched it overboard, and the cable followed it, snaking out till it came up solidly against the bitts.

The first impact of the hurricane had actually flattened the waves, raking off their tops and whirling them away in driven spray. Now the seas were building up again. The biggest waves Rod had ever seen came rushing down on the *Pelican* out of the darkness to windward. Gray-black and foam-crested, they towered mountain high, and as the ship met them she reared and plunged on her cable like a tethered horse.

All hands fought their way back to whatever places of safety they could find. Rod had just regained his hold on the shrouds when a monstrous sea loomed over the bows. It was higher than the tip of the bowsprit—higher than the foremast crosstrees. In the long, tense moment while it hung over them, the boy made a desperate attempt to climb higher on the ratlines. His fingers slipped and his legs felt paralyzed. Then a big brown hand reached down, caught him by the arm and lifted him upward. He saw the flash of Smiling Jimmy's white teeth. When the avalanche of water came over the lifting bow, Rod and the Kanaka were high enough in the shrouds to be safe.

The great wave roared aft, filling the deck, surging around the masts, crashing against the break of the poop. For a few seconds Rod thought the ship was sinking, for there was nothing left of her but her masts and rigging above the rushing flood. Then, gallantly, she fought clear, lifting to meet the next sea. There were more big waves to follow, but nothing to match that terrible mountain of water that had engulfed them.

One by one the men came down from their perches and began to take stock of the damage. One boat was gone and two others stove in. The fore topgallant mast hung in a twisted snarl of stays, slatting to and fro in the wind, which still blew with almost unabated fury. The pigpen by the try-works had gone overboard, along with its unlucky tenant.

Mike Flynn cupped his hands and bellowed loud

enough to be heard above the gale. "Stir yer stumps, there, ye lubbers! Get aloft now an' cut away that t'gallant mast!"

Three men with axes and boarding knives made their way up the rigging and managed to reach the fore crosstrees. While they were at work the first mate gathered all hands for a rollcall. Voice after voice answered down the line. It seemed incredible to Rod that nobody had been washed overboard, but Macomber had nearly completed the roll and not one was missing.

"Girty," he shouted finally. There was no reply.

"Fred Girty!" he repeated at the top of his lungs. "Anybody notice him before that sea hit us?"

There was a general shaking of heads, and the mate looked grim. "Must have gone over the side," he said. "We'll hold services for him later. Right now there's too much to do. Get at it, all of you. Stow all the loose gear you see, an' report damage to me."

Rod and Seth moved aft together, holding to the hand-lines as each fresh sea came aboard. They were both wet to the skin and shivering in the icy wind.

"Where were you when the big wave came?" Rod asked his friend through chattering teeth.

"Up for'ard. Lashed myself to the capstan. Gosh— it was a long time before I got my head out o' water!"

They picked up splintered pieces of planking from

one of the stove boats and took them to the galley. There the cook was manfully trying to get a fire going with wet wood. By a plentiful use of whale oil he finally succeeded, and in a few minutes there was hot tea and soup for the half-frozen crew.

The worst of the hurricane must have passed over, for the gale had lost some of its force. Perhaps it was this slackening in the howl of the gale, or it might have been the smell of hot food. Whatever the cause, the forecastle hatch opened suddenly and Fred Girty crawled out. He was starting to slink toward the galley when Mike Flynn spied him. With a roar of rage the stocky Irishman lunged forward. He had a marlinespike in his fist and it looked as if he meant to brain the unfortunate youth.

"Easy there," said Macomber sharply. "Let me talk to him first."

The mate collared Girty and backed him up against the foremast.

"Where've you been?" he asked.

The sailor cringed and bared his buck teeth like a cornered rat.

"I was sleepin'," he snarled. "Never heard the watch called."

"That's a lie," said Macomber. "I saw you on deck when we were snugging down before the gale hit us. You sneaked off when all hands were needed

and went below. You ought to be put in irons. 'Stead
o' that I'm sending you aloft. Get up that foremast
and help cut away the wreckage."

*   *   *

When the helmsmen were relieved, Rod was sent
aft to the wheel with Manuel, the sturdy Portuguese.
The drogue held the *Pelican's* head up and kept her
from broaching-to, but there was still plenty of work
at the helm. Gripping the spokes of the kicking
wheel was good, hard exercise, and the boy soon
stopped shivering.

Overhead, the blackness had begun to break. Torn
clouds whirled past on the wind, but the sky was
lighter, and they could see the marching gray waves
for a mile or more around them.

It was Rod who caught the first glimpse of the
wreck to starboard.

"Look!" he yelled. "Something like the mast of a
ship—over there!"

The thing he had seen vanished between two
waves for a moment, then reappeared on the crest.
The afterguard and half the crew were at the bulwarks now, staring through the spray. What they
saw was a broken stump of mast, rising from the hull
of a battered ship. She wallowed in the trough, half
swamped by every on-rushing sea. As she drifted

past, only a hundred yards away, they could see every inch of her bare deck and there was no sign of a human being aboard her. For a moment her stern lifted when she was just abeam. On her square transom they read the broken letters, "ABIGAIL SLOCUM, Nantucket."

Manuel could not read, but he recognized the shattered hulk. "Dat sheep!" he cried. "I know her. She's Nantucket whaler. All her men—dey los'!"

White and shaken by what they had seen, the crew went back to their work. Even if there had been living men aboard the wreck, they knew they would have been powerless to help them. No boat could possibly be launched in such a sea.

Silent at the wheel, Rod remembered old Matty Gage's words about the *Abigail Slocum.* He wondered what had happened. Perhaps the penny-pinching skipper and his bucko mates had driven her too long before shortening sail. Any ship with canvas on her might easily have been dismasted and rolled under by the first awful shock of the hurricane.

By nightfall, the topgallant mast of the *Pelican* had been cleared and she was as shipshape as they could make her until the storm was over. After supper the port watch was allowed to go below.

The rest of the seamen ignored Fred Girty, who sulked in his berth. They did what they could to clean up the forecastle, hung their blankets up to dry and crouched around the lamp discussing the fate of the *Abigail Slocum*. Some of the older hands disagreed with Rod's opinion.

"It wa'n't necessarily bad seamanship that lost her," said Moses Howland. "Mebbe they didn't have the makin's of a sea anchor handy. If we hadn't got ours over mighty spry we could ha' been in the same fix. You youngsters don't seem to realize how close we all come to shakin' hands with Davy Jones."

Next morning the wind was down but the sky remained overcast, and those giant seas still came tumbling out of the west. Rod heard the captain and first mate discussing the look of things.

"Glass is rising," said Macomber. "Ought to bring a spell o' fair weather by tomorrow."

"What's she read now?" asked the skipper.

" 'Most up to the twenty-nine mark," Macomber told him. "Never saw the barometer lower'n it went yesterday. Just before that black cloud reached us, 'twas down to twenty-seven point five!"

Beale nodded. "I caught it at point four," he said. "That's about as low as the glass ever goes, even in a China Sea typhoon. I've made the Cape Horn passage six times, but this was the heaviest weather I can remember."

By noon it cleared sufficiently for the mate to shoot

the sun, and as the sea gradually abated, they got topsails on the ship and hauled in the drogue.

Their drift during the storm could not have been more than a hundred miles, for on the second day following, the captain set a northwestward course. With the wind strong and steady on the port bow they beat their way up along the Chilean coast.

North of the fiftieth parallel they found warmer weather and a moderate sea. Little by little the direction of the prevailing breeze shifted into the west and they were able to make a reach of it under plain sail. There was little work for the crew aloft but plenty to be done on deck. The storm had caused a hundred kinds of damage, big and little, all over the ship. Halyards had to be spliced and stays repaired. The carpenter, with half a dozen hands to help him, worked steadily on the smashed boats, replacing oak ribs, nailing on new planking, calking sprung seams.

They had hoisted a jury spar to the fore-top and guyed it in position. The placing of a real topgallant mast would have to wait till they could anchor where they would be sheltered from wind and sea.

During the first three days of July, the *Pelican* was almost constantly in sight of land. On the eastern horizon Rod could make out the dim shapes of mountains, unbelievably high, their sides and summits cloaked in snow. His schooling, at the little one-room schoolhouse in Durham, had been limited. But the subject that had interested him most was geography, and he knew enough about South America to realize that those peaks were the Andes.

"We'll make the port o' Valparaiso tomorrow," Seth told him one night at the wheel. "I heard it right from the Old Man. An' do you know what day tomorrow is? The Fourth o' July—that's what! Maybe we'll get ashore to celebrate!"

In the middle of the morning watch, the battered old whaler drew closer to the rocky coast, rounded a headland and sent up signal flags. Within ten minutes a small sailing vessel came under her quarter and the Chilean pilot climbed aboard. Slowly they sailed into the crescent-shaped harbor. They could see the masts of a dozen ships lying at anchor, with small boats of various kinds plying between them and the shore. And rising from the beach in steep hillside terraces was the old Spanish town, the white walls of its houses gleaming in the morning sun.

IX

THEY dropped anchor between two other Yankee whalers, the *Narragansett,* out of Providence, and a New Bedford ship, the *Lancer.* The yard-arms of both vessels were draped with red-white-and-blue bunting, and aboard the *Narragansett* a little brass cannon kept firing noisy salutes.

Captain Beale had his boat lowered almost immediately. He was rowed over to the *Lancer* to talk to her skipper and give him the news of the *Abigail Slocum's* loss. The rest of the *Pelican's* crew were kept busy, however. Sails had to be harbor-furled and decks scrubbed. It was well into the afternoon before the work was done. While they were still wondering if shore leave would be granted, three boatloads of men from the *Lancer* put off and rowed across to them.

Macomber, who was in charge of the *Pelican* in the skipper's absence, welcomed them aboard. It was the first time Rod had seen a "gam," as visits between whalemen were called, and even though he was an outsider he enjoyed it to the full. Half the men in the *Pelican's* forecastle seemed to know members of the *Lancer's* crew. Their greetings were loud and exuberant, and they swarmed over the deck, laughing, slapping one another on the back, exchanging news and telling of their adventures.

The *Lancer* had been out two years and would have her hold well filled if she could capture a few more whales. In any case, she was homeward bound. Seth knew two of the younger sailors—both New Bedford boys. He introduced them to Rod and the four of them went up into the bows to get away from the hurly-burly amidships.

The first thing the visitors asked for was letters from home. When Seth replied that he had none, they were downhearted for only a moment.

"Shucks," grinned the bigger one, a lad Seth called

'Lijah, "with luck we'll be home in six months any-how. Bet you wish you were goin' with us."

"Not me," Seth told him stoutly. "We've got whales to catch. An' when you're freezing, back in New England, we'll be picking coconuts in the Islands."

'Lijah gave a raucous laugh. "We been there," he said. "Put in for water at Tonga. Got about half our casks filled an' the cannibals come a-boilin' out o' the jungle. They durn near had us for supper! I ain't so sure I want to stay home, though. Might ship out to Californy an' dig for gold."

"We heard they'd found it before we sailed," said Seth. "What's the latest news?"

"Last I heard," the other boy told him, "fellers was comin' into town with their pockets full of it. Hundreds o' dollars you can pick up in half an hour."

He lowered his voice and looked around cautiously. "We got word some o' the crew aboard the *Narragansett* are fixin' to mutiny," he whispered. "Soon as they're far enough north they aim to take over the ship an' beach her somewheres near Frisco, so they can get to the gold fields!"

At seven bells of the afternoon watch, the *Lancer's* visiting party was piped back aboard. The boys went below after supper and turned in early. Since only a harbor watch was kept, there was a chance for most of the crew to get a full night's sleep—something they hadn't enjoyed in their whole six months of voyaging.

Rod curled up luxuriously in his bunk, expecting to dream undisturbed till morning. But habit was too strong to be broken so easily. He woke at the stroke of midnight. All the men were snoring in their berths, and even the lamp above the table had guttered out. For a while he lay there, trying to go back to sleep, but the air in the forecastle was stifling. Without making any noise he went over to the ladder and climbed out on deck.

It was a dark, still night, with no moon. Rod stood by the hatch and stared aft into the blackness of the empty deck. He wondered what had become of the two men who were supposed to be on watch. One was a Portuguese named Diego. The other, he remembered, was Ben Locker. Oh, well—it wasn't his business if the pair had found some out-of-the-way corner and gone to sleep. In fact that was about what he would have expected of the Nantucketer. The other man probably didn't know any better.

Rod stretched his arms and drew in deep breaths of the fresh, cold air. He was almost ready to go below again when he heard a muffled thud, coming from somewhere beyond the dark bulk of the try-works. Then a shadowy figure darted across to the rail and vanished over the side.

For an instant the boy was too startled to move. Then he raced aft to the spot where the man had disappeared. He could hear a faint splashing a few yards off, and see a trail of phosphorescent bubbles leading away from the ship.

"Help!" he shouted at the top of his lungs. "Help! Man overboard!"

He ran to the break of the poop, flung open the hatch and yelled his message down the companion-way to rouse the afterguard.

A sound like a groan behind him made him turn. Hurrying forward once more, he came on a tumbled heap by the foot of the mainmast. It was a man, and as he drew closer Rod made out the swarthy features of Diego. There was blood on his head, blood on the deck beneath it. And a few feet away lay the marline-spike that must have been used for the blow.

He was still kneeling by the wounded Portuguese when footsteps came pounding toward him from fore and aft. The beam of a bull's-eye lantern half blinded him.

Macomber spoke. "What's up here, lad?" he asked sharply.

"Somebody went overboard," Rod choked. "I heard the splash an' saw his wake. I hollered for help an'—an' then I found Diego here, with his head bashed."

"Who had the deck watch?" the mate snapped.

"Locker, sir," mumbled several voices from the crew. "Locker an' Diego, sir."

"Well, where's Locker?"

There was an uncomfortable silence.

"All right," growled Macomber. "Lower a boat—an' be quick. We've enough for a boat's crew here. Jump to it! You, Manuel, take care o' the man that's hurt."

In a matter of seconds they had a boat in the water and Rod was at one of the oars.

"Which way'd he go?" the mate asked him.

"Last I saw him, sir, he was headed that way," he said, pointing toward the *Narragansett,* some three hundred yards away.

"Give way, men," ordered Macomber grimly. "Put your backs in it!"

They shot swiftly across the space that separated the two ships. The beam of the lantern played over the dark water and came to rest on a moving dot, close under the *Narragansett's* bow chains.

"There he is," said the mate. "Pull, boys."

They came alongside and two of the oarsmen grabbed Locker as he tried to haul himself up by a loose end of rope. Macomber collared him and dragged him aft to the sternsheets.

"All right," he commanded. "Back to the ship."

Where Rod sat, on the after-thwart, the Nantucketer was almost between his knees. Too exhausted to offer any resistance, he lay panting in the bottom of the boat with water dripping from his lank hair. In the darkness it was difficult to see his face, but there was no mistaking the hatred in his half-strangled voice.

"I'll get ye fer this, ye sneakin' dog," he croaked, and Rod knew the threat was meant for him.

They hauled Locker up to the deck and hoisted the boat in. Captain Beale, the other officers and most of the 'foremast hands were waiting for them in grim silence.

Macomber jerked the prisoner erect by the collar of his shirt, and they stood before the captain.

Beale's face was set in hard lines. "The man, Diego, is still alive," he said coldly. "But it's no thanks to you, Locker. If he dies you'll hang for it. Anything to say?"

There was no reply.

"Very well," continued the captain after a moment's wait. "Get the irons on him, Mr. Macomber, and throw him in the brig." He turned on his heel and went back to his cabin.

Early next morning the skipper went ashore in his boat to get medical help and arrange for taking on fresh water and provisions.

The doctor who returned with him was a bearded, elderly Spaniard, who could speak only a few words of English. He seemed to know a good deal about wounds, however, and he did a workmanlike job in bandaging Diego's head. Through Manuel, who served as interpreter, he assured Captain Beale that the injured Portuguese had a good chance to live, despite a fracture of the skull.

Lighters came alongside later in the day, bringing water to fill the ship's casks. Bags of onions and other vegetables also came aboard.

Meanwhile the carpenter had shaped a spar for the fore-topgallant mast and, with the weather still fair and the wind light, the crew prepared to hoist it into place. This was done with a pair of "shears" —long spars, braced together near their tops and braced to the foredeck. A second tackle was rigged from the main topgallant crosstrees to sway the new stick into position, and before dark the job was completed.

There was no shore leave that night. Most of the men were too tired to care, though a few chronic grumblers thought it was their due. When Rod woke next morning it was to a call of "All hands on deck," and in a few moments they were weighing anchor. With a freshening breeze the *Pelican* dipped her colors to the other ships and sailed out of Valparaiso harbor.

*   *   *

Rod and Seth watched the distant mountains sink into the sea astern that afternoon with mixed feelings.

"I'd have liked to set foot ashore," said Rod, "just to see how it felt—an' maybe to say I'd been in Chile."

Seth laughed. "Feels about the same as New England underfoot," he said. "An' you can still tell your grandchildren what happened in Valipo. I knew that feller, Locker, was an ornery cuss, but what d'you s'pose got into him?"

"Gold fever, I reckon," Rod replied. "He must ha' heard the same tale we did—about the *Narragansett* crowd planning to mutiny. Maybe he tried to get Diego to jump ship with him, but I doubt it. Looks to me as if he clubbed him so he wouldn't be caught. Anyhow, if I hadn't happened to come on deck he'd have got away with it. Likely nobody'd have found out till morning. He must ha' planned to stow away aboard the *'Gansett* an' join in with the mutineers later."

"Well," said the other boy, "he's sure got a grudge

against you. What'll you do when they let him out o' the brig?"

"Nothing," Rod answered soberly. "Just be careful, I guess. I wouldn't want to let him get behind me on a dark night, but he's too much of a coward to try anything in daylight, with folks around."

"You don't need to worry for a while, anyway," said Seth. "They're sure to keep him locked up till the Portygee's out o' danger. But that takes two men out o' the crew. We're going to be short-handed in the boats if we raise a whale."

"Wish they'd shift the men around an' put you in our boat," Rod laughed. "But I reckon you still think your crew is the best."

"Sure I do," said Seth stoutly. "Injun John really knows how to handle a boat, an' Matty Gage has thrown the iron into more whales than a dog has fleas."

"You think there's much chance o' whales hereabouts?" asked Rod.

His friend nodded. "Any time now," he said. "This is the 'onshore ground.' See those masthead lookouts? They know they might sight a spout any minute an' they're right on their toes."

As if to make up for the fury of the Cape Horn gale, the weather was now as fine as any sailor could ask. Day after day, as they cruised northward, the sun shone and the southeast trades blew steadily. Rod, taking his turn at the fore crosstrees, found the view clear all the way to the horizon. He kept a keen watch of the sea around him, but up to the time the lookouts were changed at noon there was nothing to break the blue expanse.

The man at the main-masthead had already started down and Rod's relief was climbing the ratlines when he took a final look before descending. Suddenly he froze to his perch, putting up a hand to shade his eyes. He thought he had seen a low, bushy cloud of vapor on the surface of the sea. It was a mile or more to the northwest—a white cloud that looked no bigger than a thimble at that distance.

He drew a deep breath and gave a triumphant yell —"Blows! Ah—bl-o-o-w-s! Two points on the port bow!"

"Are ye sure, boy?" came Mike Flynn's call from the deck.

"Spout's gone now, sir," Rod answered. "But it was there all right. An' a sparm whale, too."

"Ye *better* be sure," bawled the second mate. "If we lower fer nothin', I'll have the hide off ye!"

Three minutes later the boats had been put over the side and the men were digging in with their oars. Macomber had drafted Asa Tetlow, the cooper, to replace Locker on the stern thwart. He was a strong, slow-moving man, grizzled with age, but when he bent his back to it he pulled a powerful stroke. The boat held its own in the race toward the spot Rod had indicated.

"Ah, blows!" shouted Smiling Jimmy, in the bows, and Macomber, stretching to his full height, nodded eagerly to the rowers.

"Give way, boys!" he urged. "He's right ahead— not more'n a dozen boat-lengths—an' we've got to beat Flynn's men to get in the first iron!"

They pulled like madmen, lifting the light hull half out of water. If Fred Girty hadn't caught a crab with his oar at the last minute, the Kanaka harpooner would have had a clean shot. As it was, the boat fell off just enough to spoil his aim, and he had to haul in his line. Meanwhile the giant Lucifer drove his iron deep into the whale's side and the second mate's crew roared their triumph.

"Port oars astarn!" cried Macomber. "Sheer off— it's not sounding! Must be a fighting whale!"

The hasty response of the rowers spun the boat sidewise and Rod stole a terrified glance over his shoulder. What he expected to see was the whale's head with its saw-toothed open jaw, or—equally dangerous—the great flukes raised on high. To his amazement the huge beast lay there quietly, the upper third of its body above the waves.

"Cow whale!" yelled Smiling Jimmy. "Look-um baby!"

Staring over the gunwale, Rod could make out a small dark shadow clinging close to the mother whale's side. There was something about the scene that made his heart ache. The cow made no effort to escape or to defend herself. Her single purpose seemed to be to protect her little calf.

In the second mate's boat, Flynn had scrambled forward to change places with the big Negro. He braced his stocky leg into the kneehole, coolly lifted his lance and plunged it with all his strength into the motionless whale's vitals. There was no flurry. She gave a last gasping spout and the spray was red with her blood.

"Never mind the calf," shouted Flynn. "He wouldn't try out a barrel of oil all told. Get a line around the flukes an' we'll tow her in."

The first mate's boat also attached a rope to the dead whale's tail and with both crews pulling they made good time back to the ship. Even when the big carcass was made fast alongside, Rod could see the baby swimming forlornly back and forth, nuzzling occasionally against its mother's belly. For the first time the boy had a sick feeling about whaling. It seemed to him a beastly business.

The cutting stages and tackles were quickly rigged,

and the harpooners went to work with their spades. By ten o'clock that night the last of the blubber was tried out and the stripped body had been cast off to drift astern. Rod wondered, as he lay in his bunk that night, whether the orphaned calf still clung to that bleeding hulk, or whether it had already been torn to pieces by the sharks that were devouring the dead whale. It was a long time before he could forget his unhappiness in sleep.

# X

THE HELMSMAN was given a fresh course next day, and the *Pelican* boomed westward under full sail. With the steady push of the trade winds behind her, she was on the "offshore ground" before the week had passed.

A keen watch was kept aloft, for this was one of the finest whaling waters in the world. Meanwhile the harpooners whetted their irons to razor sharpness, the mates inspected every inch of whale line, and Chips, the carpenter, worked daily on the boats and gear.

Locker was still confined to the brig, for though Diego had regained consciousness, he was so weak that no man could say whether he would live or die.

Among the other men of the crew Rod had achieved quite a reputation as a lookout, after twice sighting whales. Some even spoke of him as "the luck of the ship"—high praise indeed from whalemen. But it was not his fortune to be aloft when the next sperm was sighted.

The long-expected hail came just after daybreak one morning toward the end of July. The sailor at the mainmast head gave the first excited yell.

"Thar she blows! Right to loo-ard—'bout three mile. Sparm whale—two of 'em—no—five—six— it's a whole pod of 'em an' a big 'un!"

His news was verified by the man in the fore crosstrees. "I count twenty spouts!" he whooped. "Biggest pod o' whales I ever see!"

Captain Beale was on deck in a jiffy, ordering all hands to man the boats. There was no time for breakfast, but they were too excited to think of that. In a little more than a minute all four boat crews had lowered away and tumbled to their places. No sooner had they pulled clear of the ship than their leg-o'- mutton sails were hoisted and they went skimming down before the wind, heading for the spot where the whales had been sighted.

There was no sign of a spout as they drew near, for the pod had sounded. One by one the boats furled their sails and unstepped the masts. Nobody shouted or talked. Ezra Macomber stood tall at the steering oar and signaled the other boats with gestures of his hands. At his order they spread out over the long, easy swells till they drifted at least a cable's length apart.

They rested on their oars, waiting. The minutes dragged by. After what seemed to Rod at least half an hour, he began wondering whether the whales would ever come up again. Perhaps they had been "gallied" by the noise of the approaching boats. In that case they might be miles away by now, swimming under the sea in any direction that took their fancy.

Just as he was making up his mind that this had happened there was a sudden swirling of water a hundred feet from the boat's side. Then an enormous black back broke the surface. The whale rose lazily and lolled there, half submerged, apparently unconscious of any danger. With a sound like a vast sigh a cloud of steamy vapor rushed from the spout hole at the top of the great, square head.

The crew needed no word of command to send them into action. As one man they dug deep with their oars, swinging the bow toward the whale. Smiling Jimmy's white teeth flashed as he gripped the shaft of his iron and crooned a little Kanaka tune under his breath.

They had taken two or three strokes and covered about half the distance to the whale when their whole world seemed to fly apart. Something came up under the keel, striking the boat with a terrifying crash. The oar was jolted out of Rod's hands and he felt himself catapulted into space, whirling over and over as he went. There was a roaring in his ears. He caught glimpses of grotesquely twisted bodies and splintered fragments of the boat, all tossed upward with him.

Then he was falling. He struck the water heavily and went down and down. The shock and the cold made him helpless at first, but the ache in his lungs forced him to swim. He clawed desperately upward. After an endless time his head came out of water and he gulped a mouthful of air. With a kind of wonder he knew that he was alive.

Fortunately the warmer weather of the northward passage had given the crew a chance to discard their winter clothes. In sea boots and reefers most of them would have sunk like stones. As it was, Rod wore nothing but a shirt and dungarees. He was a good swimmer and found no trouble in keeping himself afloat.

Around him in the water were bobbing heads, drifting oars and pieces of wreckage. The whale that had hit them was nowhere in sight, and the first one—the one they had been attacking—had also disappeared.

He saw Ezra Macomber, a few feet away, a wry grin on his long Yankee face. Then he heard a choking cry behind him. Treading water, he turned in time to see Asa Tetlow's head go under. With a sinking heart he remembered that the cooper had once told him he could not swim.

Rod's arms flailed the water as he tried to reach the drowning man. But before he had taken two strokes a lithe brown body flashed past him. Smiling Jimmy, as much at home in the water as a fish, seized Tetlow by the hair and dragged him to the surface. The big Kanaka swam easily, holding the other man's face out of water with a hand on each side of his head.

Macomber waited till he was on the crest of a swell and jumped as high as he could.

"Boat's comin'," he panted, shaking the water out of his eyes. "Everybody hang on an' we'll be picked up."

Looking around him Rod could count all seven members of the boat's crew. Manuel and the other Portuguese were floating near him, holding on to the boat's mast, and Fred Girty had found one of the line tubs to use as a support.

Their rescuers seemed a long time in coming but at last they hove in sight. The boat was the one commanded by Sanchez, the third mate. It pulled alongside and one at a time they were hauled, dripping, over the gunwale.

As soon as space could be made in the crowded boat, Macomber laid the unconscious Tetlow across a thwart and proceeded to roll the salt water out of him. After a minute or two the cooper's eyes opened and he managed to draw a choking breath. Then the first mate stood erect, scanning the sea.

The great pod of whales had vanished, but the other two boats were visible, half a mile away, and behind each of them trailed a long, dark bulk.

"Two whales," said the mate briefly. "That'll make up for the stove boat. Let's get on back to the ship, Sanchez."

They were a glum lot as they pulled up under the lee of the *Pelican*. Captain Beale tucked his spyglass under his arm and leaned over the rail.

"What happened, Mr. Macomber?" he asked.

"Whale breached under us," replied the mate. "Knocked our boat to smithereens. No men lost. If you'll let us, sir, I'd like to take this boat with my crew an' give the others a hand."

The captain agreed, and ten minutes later Rod and his boat-mates were fast to the larger of the two whales, captured by Injun John's crew. They took some good-natured ribbing from the men in the fourth mate's boat, and had very little to say in return.

The cutting-stages were soon rigged and the harpooners began the bloody job of cutting-in. Working at the tackle, Rod could look over the side and see the big gray sharks gathering to the feast. During those minutes when he had been in the water, the thought of sharks had never crossed his mind. Now he shuddered in horror at the thought of what might have happened.

"Gosh," he muttered, turning to Moses Howland, who was pulling the rope beside him. "Where do they come from? There must be thousands of 'em swimming around us all the time—an' yet they didn't come near when the boat got smashed out there. I can't figure it."

"It's the blood," the big seaman replied. "Sharks can smell it for miles. If one o' you fellers had got a scratch—bled even a spoonful—you'd ha' been eaten in a jiffy. But if there's no blood around, a man don't need to worry much. You just thrash the water with your arms an' they'll sheer off."

By noon their morning mishap was forgotten, with every man working at top speed to get the blubber aboard. One whale was finished before midnight, but the second took them well into the next day. When they finally tumbled, exhausted, into their bunks, a hundred and sixty barrels of sperm oil had been added to the cargo.

*　　*　　*

Rod was alone at the wheel when Macomber shot the sun, one August noon a few days later.

"Getting close to the Line," the mate reported to Beale. "I make it three degrees south, an' about one-forty-eight west."

The skipper scratched his chin. "That puts us just a bit over a thousand miles from the Sandwich Islands," he said. "With good weather we could reach Hilo in less than two weeks. How's Chips coming with a new boat?"

"He's making slow progress," Macomber answered. "Most of his lumber was used for repairs after the Cape Horn storm."

"All right," said the captain. "To Hilo it is. There'll be other ships in harbor and we can buy a boat or get one built. How's our course?"

"Fair as she is," said Macomber, casting an eye aloft at the draw of the sails. "Maybe one point more to sta'board if you like."

"Hear that, helmsman?" the captain called. "Bring her up a point."

"Aye, aye, sir," Rod replied and turned the wheel obediently. "The Islands!" he thought to himself. "Palm trees an' coconuts! Wait till the boys in the fo'c'sle hear that!"

When he was relieved he lost no time in finding Smiling Jimmy, lolling in the shade of the main-mast, sharpening a new harpoon to replace the one he had lost.

"*Aloha!*" he greeted the Kanaka in his own tongue. "Guess where we're bound, Jimmy. Right now we're pointed up for your home island—Hawaii—an' the port o' Hilo! Be there in a couple o' weeks, the cap'n says."

The big brown man's eyes widened and his white teeth gleamed in a grin.

"Me-fella plenty glad," he said. "You come 'long me-fella, me show you plenty fine place. Eat-um fish an' *poi*—mebbe-so go to *luau*—eat an' sing an' dance all night!"

He chattered on, using so many native phrases that Rod was soon out of his depth. But the boy understood the drift of the conversation. Smiling Jimmy was promising to show him the sights of the Islands. He resolved then and there to learn as many Hawaiian words as he could, so that he would be able to ask questions and understand the answers, if and when he got ashore.

In the next few days he found plenty of opportunity to study the language with his Kanaka friend. As they neared the equator the trade winds died out and the ship rolled sluggishly, unable to keep steerageway. While the other men loafed about the deck, trying to stay out of the blazing sun, Rod made good progress with the Hawaiian tongue. First he asked Smiling Jimmy the names of simple, everyday things, then went on to the verbs and action words. It wasn't always easy, for he discovered the Kanaka's vocabulary was limited. Many of the words seemed to be nothing more than oddly-pronounced imitations of English, as in fact they were. The Islanders had picked up phrases from the missionaries and seamen and adapted them to their own liquid way of speech.

They were becalmed for three days. On the fourth afternoon the sky grew dark in the south and all hands hurried aloft to shorten sail. The tropical storm overtook them just before sunset and they were driven all night before a furious wind. But not a man in the crew complained, for the gale was carrying them northward, away from the doldrums that had plagued them on the Line.

When the storm blew itself out there was another

day of light, uncertain air. Then they woke one morning to bright skies and a cool, steady breeze from the northeast. They had found the trades once more.

Close-hauled, the *Pelican* made her northerly passage, logging a steady hundred and twenty miles each day. It was midway in the first dog watch, eight days after the storm, that the masthead lookout sighted land. At his excited hail Rod started aloft as fast as he could climb, but for all his agility Smiling Jimmy was at the top of the fore-shrouds ahead of him. The Kanaka thrust out a long brown arm, pointing to the horizon off the port bow.

"Mauna Kea!" he cried exultantly. And Rod, staring in that direction, saw a gray mass, topped with a fringe of white, rising from the far rim of the sea.

To the boy it seemed that they must surely reach the island before morning, but Ezra Macomber told him later that it would take another full day's sailing.

"Those mountains are mighty high," the mate said. "When they're in eruption you can see the smoke, an' the red in the sky at night, for four or five hundred miles. Last time I saw Mauna Loa blow her top was in 'forty-three."

Gradually, as the next day passed, the bulk of the twin volcanos lifted higher on the horizon. They could see black masses of lava along their sloping sides below the snow-crested summits. Then, still farther down, the green of forests appeared, and at last the white line of surf along the eastern coast.

It was nearly sunset when they made the entrance to Hilo harbor. Sheets were slacked and they started to run in before the wind. Rod, up forward by the rail, heard old Matty Gage give an exclamation of surprise.

"That's a funny thing," the veteran whaleman said. "Not a durn ship in port. What in tarnation—say, ain't that a warnin' flag over the harbor master's buildin'?"

At that moment there was a brisk command from the quarterdeck. "All hands to come about!" shouted the captain. "Lively now, if you want to stay healthy. Looks like they've got cholera here."

Rod's heart was heavy as he pulled on the halyards. He looked around for Smiling Jimmy but the harpooner was nowhere in sight. Perhaps, the boy thought, the Kanaka had seen the signal flag and gone below to hide his disappointment. He waited for him on deck after the watch was changed, but his friend did not appear. At last he went to his berth in the forecastle. It was difficult to go to sleep, for he kept thinking of Smiling Jimmy's radiant face when he heard they were to put in at his home island.

Through the night the *Pelican* tacked out to windward till she was well clear of the reefs and lay hoveto, waiting for daylight. Then, all morning long, they sailed northwestward along the Hamakua Coast of the island of Hawaii. Clouds lay above the vivid green of the jungle and frequent showers hid the shore. Then the mists would lift to give them glimpses of waterfalls, tumbling like white ribbons down the cliffs. And every few minutes they saw the arch of a brilliant rainbow hanging in the sky above the mountaintops.

Rod was admiring the wild beauty of the scene when Ezra Macomber came striding forward.

"Any of you seen Jimmy, the harpooner?" he asked. "He didn't sleep in his bunk in the steerage last night."

There was no answer, and the mate went aft again, a worried look on his face. Rod kept silence, but he had a clear mental picture of his friend back there in Hilo, squatting cross-legged before a big bowl of *poi,* and being greeted by brown-skinned men and maidens. Somewhere near the harbor mouth he must have slipped quietly over the side and made for the shore, swimming with that long, powerful, over-arm stroke of his.

XI

THEY made a long reach of it to the west and northwest, cutting through Alenuihaha Channel between the Big Island and Maui, where the ramparts of Haleakala towered out of the sea. One after another, new islands appeared to starboard— first little Kahoolawe, then Lanai and Molokai. At dawn of the third day after leaving Hilo, they sighted Diamond Head and came in past the beaches to the anchorage in Honolulu Harbor.

It was a fine, clear morning. Blue waves slapped and chuckled around the *Pelican's* forefoot as she threaded her way through the moored ships, and before they could drop anchor a swarm of outrigger canoes came skimming out to meet them. Each slender craft was manned by laughing islanders who guided it skillfully with oval-bladed paddles. They were handsome people—men and women, boys and girls—with wreaths of flowers around their necks or single blossoms tucked in their hair. Crowding close to the ship's side they jabbered friendly greetings to the sailors along the rail and held up coconuts, small brown bananas, and other fruits whose names Rod did not know.

Captain Beale waved them sternly away. "Clear out, now," he ordered. "We'll have no visitors aboard here. Go take your stuff somewhere else."

The natives showed no resentment but laughed and paddled away. For the next hour the crew was kept on the jump, furling sails, putting over anchors fore and aft, and stowing gear. Then, at last, they had a chance to look around them.

The roadstead was full of shipping. A dozen whalers and half as many merchantmen rocked gently at their moorings, tall masts and spars and rigging making a spidery pattern against the sky.

The New Bedford men picked out ships they knew—the *Heron* and the *Prudence* from Nantucket, the *Rorqual, Sea Lion, Yankee, Lightning* and *Abner*

L. Chase from New Bedford, and the *Blackfish* from Sag Harbor. Rod, with less interest in the vessels, was staring with rapt attention at the town, and the island of Oahu.

On the low land near the docks he could see clusters of white buildings and a church spire or two. Above them loomed a wall of green. And still higher, his eyes traveled up to the jagged, dark summits of volcanic mountains.

Shortly after the noonday meal the captain ordered his boat lowered. As he stood by the rail, preparing to go down the ladder, he turned to the assembled crew.

"There'll be a chance for all hands to go ashore tomorrow," he said. "Anybody who tries to leave the ship before then will be brought back and put in irons."

When Beale returned he brought a doctor with him and they went aft at once to look at the wounded sailor, Diego. Apparently the medico's diagnosis was not very hopeful. He was shaking his head when he reappeared on deck, and the captain's face was grim. Later in the afternoon a police officer and two men came aboard and arrested Ben Locker. The Nantucket man looked defiant as they led him toward the rail. He glanced around at his shipmates with a sneer on his lips but said nothing. There were no farewells. Not a man aboard was sorry to see him go.

The sun went down behind Barber's Point and the tropic night fell swiftly. Rod and Seth sat together on a coiled cable in the bows and enjoyed the cool breeze that blew over Diamond Head. The lights of fishermen's torches flickered along the shore toward Waikiki.

"Listen," Rod murmured. "There's some kind o' music over there."

They could hear a soft throb of drums and a muted chant from somewhere in the palm grove back of the beach. Then a woman's voice, sweet and sad, rose clearly above the others. The strange, wailing notes of the song sent a shiver of delight down Rod's spine. This was different from any music he had ever heard.

"Don't think much of it," Seth remarked. "Sounds sort of outlandish to me." He yawned, stretched and wandered aft.

Rod stayed where he was, held by the spell of the singing. He was disappointed at the New Bedford boy's reaction but he supposed a taste for weird music was too much to expect from a lad with Seth's strict Quaker upbringing. Other voices joined in the chorus—men's and women's voices in perfect harmony. And now the melody that floated over the water had a familiar sound. The words were strange but there was no mistaking the tune. It was the old hymn, *Rock of Ages,* sung with a simple fervor that brought a lump into Rod's throat.

The music went on for a long time. There were savage war chants, tender love songs and missionary hymns, all sung with what seemed to be equal enjoyment.

Rod could have sat listening for hours, but other sounds rose from the docks and drowned out the singers. A crowd of sailors, some of them riotously drunk, came swarming out of the bars and down to their boats. A fight must have started between men of different crews, for in addition to their yells there was a furious barking of dogs and shrilling of bosuns' whistles. Finally the uproar died down and boats began straggling past, hunting their ships in the darkness.

In the forecastle, the boy found the rest of the watch asleep or bragging about the sprees they would have in Honolulu when they landed tomorrow. The talk sickened him. He wanted to go ashore as much as any of them, but for a different reason. Instead of spending his time in saloons he meant to see as much of this enchanted island as he possibly could.

*   *   *

It was ten o'clock before the first boat was allowed
to put off. Mike Flynn had made them work like
beavers from the crack of dawn, cleaning up the
ship. Then at last the crew got into their best shore-
going clothes and lined up for orders. The mates
picked half a dozen men to stay aboard as ship-
keepers and they were a glum lot. Seth was one of
them. He looked at Rod with a long face, then
grinned philosophically.

"It's all right with me," he said. "I don't hanker
to get drunk, an' I wouldn't know what to do with
myself in town anyhow."

Flynn, red-faced and puffing, was sending the
boats off. "Stay sober, ye spalpeens," he bawled.
"Keep out o' fights an' be back aboard by ten o'clock
or ye'll have me to reckon with. Any man that shows
up with a black eye will get another from me own
fist!"

Most of the men in the boat had made purchases
from the slop chest. There were several pairs of
tight new shoes that made their owners wince at
every step. Some had on bright shirts of striped
jersey, and nearly all wore shiny glazed hats with
flat brims and crowns.

Rod felt a little ashamed of his own scant attire
when he looked at all this finery. He had on a clean
shirt, open at the throat, and a pair of shabby but

well-washed dungarees, with his fine sheath-knife strapped to the belt. But his feet and his head were bare.

Old Matty Gage grinned and smacked his toothless gums as they rowed shoreward. "You fellers better steer clear o' them wahinnies," he advised. "That's the Island name fer women. You get tangled up with one of 'em an' first thing you know you'll be logged fer jumpin' ship—not to mention the chance her husband may ketch up with you."

One of the younger seamen laughed at him. "Sour grapes!" he replied. "No *wahine* would look at you anyhow, old-timer. What I want is a swig o' that likker they call 'koolyhow.'"

"If you're smart," Rufus Coffin put in, "you'll stick to drinks you can handle. I never tried the stuff myself, but I've seen more'n one sailor go plumb crazy after a gulp o' that native rotgut."

They tied up to a rickety pier and the men tumbled over each other in their eagerness to get ashore. Rod's first glimpse of the town of Honolulu came as a blow to all his imaginings. From the docks a street led back across the flats, lined on both sides by squat wooden buildings, most of them sadly in need of paint. They housed saloons, ship chandlers' shops and shabby boarding-places. Pigs rooted in the mud of the unpaved thoroughfare, and a reek of old fish and decayed vegetable matter hung in the breeze.

Disheartened, the boy wandered on up the street. All his companions had disappeared into the water-front bars and he was alone. In front of Captain Hackfeld's store, on Queen Street, he stopped to watch the passers-by. There were a few white men, preoccupied with their affairs, but most of the people in sight were brown-skinned islanders. They were a happy lot—big, lazy-looking men, naked above the waist—stout matrons in long, shapeless Mother Hubbards—and barefooted girls who giggled and rolled their dark eyes at the young seaman.

A short distance beyond he saw trees and a dooryard with a hedge of bright flowers. He moved in that direction, and suddenly, as he passed the next corner, the whole aspect of the town changed. To his left were rows of grass-thatched native houses, set among small vegetable patches and shaded by palm and banana and monkey-pod trees. On the right stood more pretentious dwellings. Some of them were two-story affairs, built in the style of sea captains' houses at home, and they were surrounded by fine lawns and gardens where flowers of many colors bloomed.

Rod stopped in front of one of these residences to stare openmouthed at a giant banyan tree with scores of smooth gray trunks rising into the dense foliage above. Just in front of him was a hedge loaded with red hibiscus blossoms. He put out his hand hesitantly and picked one of the huge flowers, half expecting a cry of "Stop, thief!" But nobody in sight paid any attention to his action, and a moment later he was relieved to see an old Hawaiian woman pluck a blossom and stick it casually in her hair.

Carrying his flower, he turned northeastward into a narrow lane that climbed gradually toward the *pali,* the high, dark mountain ridge behind the town.

After a while the houses lay far below him and the thick forest shut in on either side of the trail. He moved through cool, leafy shadows, reveling in the feel of moist earth under his bare feet. It was good to be on land again. He listened to the twittering of birds and the rustle of leaves. Somewhere near him among the trees and vines and great, green ferns he could hear a stream tumbling over rocks. A craving for fresh water seized him and he plunged into the jungle.

Moving through that wall of vegetation was harder than he had expected. It took him ten or fifteen minutes to fight his way through to the stream. As he came out on the banks a horse snorted softly a few feet away. He looked up, startled, and saw the animal standing tied to a tree. It wore an odd-shaped saddle, but its rider was nowhere to be seen.

Rod knelt by the brookside and drank thirstily, dipping his face deep in the cold, clear water. He was getting to his feet once more when he heard a little scream down the hill to his right. He turned quickly. A few yards from where he stood the brook ran over a ledge and fell into a pool that was just visible beyond. He caught a fleeting glimpse of a lovely, wide-eyed face and a flash of golden skin. Then the apparition was gone.

In some embarrassment he realized that he had surprised a young girl bathing in the pool.

"I—I won't look!" he blurted out. "I'll go away." And in blushing haste he started to claw a path back toward the road. Then he remembered that his English words would mean nothing to the girl. He stopped, trying to think of a Hawaiian phrase that might serve for an apology, but none of the words he had learned from Smiling Jimmy seemed to fit this occasion.

When he emerged on the roadside he found his hibiscus flower still lying where he had dropped it. For a moment he stood there confused, half tempted to go back and offer the girl the great red bloom to make up for having frightened her. By this time she probably had her clothes on. But a wave of shyness overcame him again and he started off, up the steep, winding road. A hundred feet higher he passed a narrow path that cut back to the right, and saw fresh hoof-prints leading into it. That explained how the horse had reached the stream bank through the jungle.

Another half hour of climbing brought Rod out on a grassy shelf below the looming cliffs. He sat down to rest. A waterfall that was hardly more than a white thread came twisting down from the high crags, losing itself in rainbow-tinted mist above the forest.

Somewhere down the trail a pebble clinked. Then he heard steady hoofbeats drawing nearer. He stood up and waited, breathing fast, an unaccustomed warmth in his cheeks. And in a moment the horse and rider reached the shelf beside him.

It was the girl from the pool, decently clad now, looking down at him with a mocking twinkle in her eyes. She was even prettier than he had thought. Her wavy hair was dark and hung in masses on her shoulders. She had a straight little nose and full, red lips, and her skin—lighter than most Hawaiians' —had a warm, golden tinge that seemed to catch and hold the sunlight.

"*Aloha!*" Rod stammered. It was the only Kanaka word he could think of at the moment.

"*Aloha,*" she replied, and followed the greeting with a flood of island speech that left him com-

pletely beyond his depth. The expression on her face made him realize he was being scolded and he had no way to answer.

Suddenly she laughed. "Don't look so miserable!" she exclaimed in English. "I know you weren't to blame. My name's Mahina Kea. What's yours?"

He stared at her, astonished. "Gosh," he breathed. "I'm sorry. I just went in there for a drink o' water an' didn't know you were around. My name's Rodney Glenn. But—you talk English better'n I do. I thought you were an Island girl—a *wahine.*"

She tossed her head back in merry laughter. "Why not?" she said. "My mother is. My father's Scotch— Robert MacNair. He owns a shipyard down by the bay. From your accent I'd say you're a whaler from New England."

"That's right," Rod told her. "Ship *Pelican,* out o' New Bedford. I'm—say, do you mind if—I'd like to give you this." With an impulsive gesture he held up the hibiscus blossom.

"*Mahalo o oe,*" she smiled. "Thank you." She twisted the stem into her hair and swung down gracefully from the saddle. Standing beside him she was tall and slender, her eyes almost level with his own.

"How old are you, Rodney?" she asked, and

when he told her she nodded. "Just my age. Do you really want to climb the *pali?*"

"Not very much. It was just for something to do—to see as much of the island as I could. We have to be back aboard by ten tonight, an'—well, I don't like hanging around grogshops."

The girl's eyes were soft and understanding. "There's a fine view up there," she said. "But it's a hard climb, even on horseback, and the wind blows like fury when you get to the top. If you want to see Oahu—the real Oahu—I know a better way."

Her white teeth flashed in a laugh. "Come on with me," she cried. "We're going to a *hukilau!*"

XII

THAT was an afternoon that Rod would never forget as long as he lived. Mahina Kea—her name, he discovered, meant "White Moon"—was as friendly as any boy, a perfect companion for such a holiday. And she saw to it that he got a true picture of Hawaiian life.

They rode double down the Nuuanu trail, Rod perched behind the saddle on the horse's rump. Once or twice the girl stopped to point out places below them—the green crater of the Punchbowl and the beach, sweeping around to Diamond Head.

The MacNair house was on the lower side of the
Punchbowl hill, facing the harbor. It was a big,
low structure, shaded by monkey-pod trees, with a
broad *lanai,* or open porch, on the windward side.
The girl introduced Rod to her mother, a tall, stately
Hawaiian woman whose pleasant smile and beautiful
manners made him feel instantly at ease. It was not
until a long time later that he learned she was of
royal blood—a cousin of King Kamehameha III—
but even at their first meeting he knew she was no
ordinary lady.

While he chatted with her in English, Mahina
Kea went off to change from her riding habit to a
simple white *muumuu,* the missionary dress worn by
most Hawaiian girls. When she returned they were
served papayas and green coconuts, and Rod had his
first delicious drink of coconut milk.

"Come on," the girl laughed, holding out her hand.
"If we stay here too long we'll miss the *hukilau.*"

They walked down past the outskirts of the town
and skirted a great meadow where Hawaiians were
racing their horses. In an hour they came to a grove
of palm trees that bordered the beach. Ahead of
them they could hear shouting and laughter, and as
they came through the trees they saw a crowd of
young people gathered on a patch of coral rock that
jutted out into the sea. Offshore there were five or

six outrigger canoes, manned by husky Kanaka boys clad only in breech-clouts.

"They're spreading the net now," Mahina Kea explained. "They make a big circle with it first and then pull the two ends ashore with those ropes."

There was plenty of merriment, on the rocks and in the water, as the canoemen dived overboard, freed the net from jagged points of coral, and tried to keep the frightened fish inside the enclosure.

"Huki!" yelled the crews of the outriggers. "Pull!" And immediately the boys and girls on shore seized the ropes and began hauling. Rod and Mahina Kea were in the thick of it, whooping with excitement as they dragged in the heavy net.

It was nearly sunset when the last few yards of net were drawn ashore and the mass of squirming, flopping fish taken from its folds. Up in the grove, cook-fires had been prepared and stones were being heated. As darkness fell the whole party squatted under the palms and began their torchlight feast.

The fish, wrapped in green leaves and cooked on hot stones, had a wonderful flavor, Rod discovered. But the *poi,* served in halves of coconut shell, was disappointing. It was a thick, sourish, gray-white paste that needed something—salt, he thought—to make it palatable.

Mahina Kea laughed at him. "No *malihini* ever

likes *poi* the first time," she said. "But it's awfully good for you. If you stayed here long enough you'd get to love it."

Rod tried manfully to imitate her, dipping a finger in the bowl and sucking the viscous stuff off, but it took a real effort to swallow it.

When everybody had eaten to the full, the singing started. Small drums, beaten with the hands, were brought out, and one of the young men played a wailing minor tune on a reed pipe. Then the girls rose and began to dance. To Rod's astonishment his pretty companion slipped out of her long, white outer garment and stood beside him in a native skirt of *ti*-leaves. About her neck and covering her breast was a huge double *lei* of white ginger flowers that gave off an intoxicating fragrance. As she stepped into the torchlit circle her slim hands and swaying body took up the beat of the chant, moving with the natural grace of a bird in flight.

To the fascinated Yankee boy she was the most beautiful thing he had ever seen, and her *hula* dance was pure magic. He swayed in rhythm with the others, joining his voice to the chorus, but his eyes never left the golden-skinned girl. He was too bemused to notice the passage of time. When at last she came back to him, laughing and breathless, and told him he must go, *wikiwiki,* to catch the boat, it was like waking from a dream.

They walked together, barefoot, through the soft Pacific night. When they came within sight of the port she stopped and held out her hand.

"Did you like it, Rod?" she asked, low-voiced. "I did. And I hope you'll come back."

There was a strange huskiness in the boy's throat that made it hard to speak. "I can't tell you how—how wonderful it was," he said. "But if I'm alive, you know I'll come back. Thank you for—for everything!"

A moment later he was running down the dark street toward the docks. He didn't feel the muddy ruts under his feet, or the gentle sprinkle of rain borne in by the trade wind. All he knew was that he had just been kissed by the loveliest girl in this or any other island.

*   *   *

"How'd you kill time ashore?" Seth asked him the next morning. "All the rest o' the boys are sick as dogs, but you seem to be uncommon spry."

"Oh," said Rod airily, "I made out pretty fair. Went up on the side o' the mountain for a look around an' then over to Waikiki, where they were having some sort of a picnic."

He described the *hukilau* in considerable detail, and the other boy appeared satisfied.

"Guess I was just as well off staying aboard," he remarked. "That *poi* stuff sounds pretty awful. I'll stick to hard-tack an' salt horse, myself."

To make up for their holiday, Flynn worked the crew mercilessly through the next few days. They took on fresh water and several sacks of sweet potatoes. For the officers' table there was a side of newly killed beef, coconuts and papayas. From MacNair's shipyard the Captain purchased a new whaleboat and several spare spars.

Rod worked with all his might, hoping the crew would be rewarded by another shore leave. But on the fifth night in port he heard Ezra Macomber say they would weigh anchor in the morning. The news hit the boy hard. Up to that moment he had been living in a kind of fool's paradise, sure that he would have at least one more chance to see Mahina Kea.

Now he faced one of the toughest decisions of his life. He had the deck watch from midnight till four, and it would not be too difficult to slide overboard and swim for shore. On the other hand, he had cast his lot with the *Pelican*. When he signed the ship's papers he had given his word to serve for the voyage, and a man's word was a matter of honor. Something told him that neither Robert MacNair nor his gracious wife would have much respect for a ship-jumping sailor as a companion for their daughter. In the end he went below when eight bells were struck, and crawled miserably into his bunk.

Sleepless and hollow-eyed, he came on deck again at the call of "All hands." With the rest he stumbled around the capstan, hauling in cable. And when the anchors were catted he went numbly aloft to loosen the furled sails. It wasn't until the *Pelican* was standing out of the harbor to round Diamond Head that he brought himself to look back at the shore. Up on the side of Punchbowl hill there was a white dot that might be the MacNair house. He stared at it with a heart full of unhappiness until Flynn's bull voice shook him out of his brooding.

"Get aloft, you Glenn!" the second mate roared. "Take the foremast lookout. There's whalin' to be done!"

It was a fine, clear day and he could see the green slopes leading up the Nuuanu Pali long after they had tacked out past the Head. Then they caught the breeze abeam, reaching to the northwest along the windward coast of Oahu. By late afternoon they had laid the island astern.

Rod sighted no whales during his watch aloft, but the clean breeze blew the bitterness out of him.

They held their course through the night and when morning dawned there was another mountainous island on the horizon over the port bow.

"Reckon that's Kauai," Matty Gage announced. "Last o' the Sandwich Islands. You ain't likely to sight land again till we git to the coast o' Japan."

They left the blue peaks of Kauai a dozen miles to leeward and sailed on through the morning. It was a few minutes past noon when Seth, who had just mounted to the main top, gave the exultant yell that sent them hurrying to the boats.

"Where away?" shouted the captain.

"Three points on the sta'board bow. 'Bout a mile off. Only one spout, but it's a big 'un!"

With Smiling Jimmy gone there had been a re-shuffling of harpooners. The giant Negro, Lucifer, now occupied the bow of the first mate's boat, and Moses Howland had been promoted to act as harpooner under Flynn. Rod replaced Asa Tetlow at the stroke oar.

They were first over the side and took a boat's length lead as they pulled away from the ship. The mast was quickly stepped, and with Rod holding the sheet they scudded along close-hauled to windward.

"He ain't sounded yit," Lucifer's deep voice rumbled. "Ah kin see his spout—dead ahead!"

"Maybe we can reach him while he's still blowing," said Macomber. "Out oars there, boys, an' put some spring into it!"

With the rowers pulling for all they were worth, and the breeze helping them along, the boat fairly skimmed over the water.

"Steady now," the mate murmured after a few minutes. "Slack off on the sheet, Glenn. You, Manuel, be ready to ship the mast. We're getting close."

The other boats were some distance astern as they drove in on their quarry. Lucifer balanced himself in the bow, his knee in the crotch, and fondly handled the shaft of the harpoon.

"Ah's gwine nail you, Mistuh Sparm," he crooned. "You's big an' tough, all right—bigges' bull Ah ever seen—but wait till you gits mah iron in yo' belly!"

Rod stole a glance over his shoulder and saw the monster only a hundred feet ahead. They were coming in just behind the great hill of the whale's hump. And to the boy's amazement, that hump was not black but grayish white. Twice more they reached, bending their backs, and twice they straightened to the pull.

"Starn all!" Macomber whispered fiercely. "Let him have it, Lucifer!"

They heard the black man let out his breath in a

hoarse, panting "Huh!" And the harpoon plunged into the whale's side till it was over the hitches and halfway up the hickory shaft.

" 'Ware flukes!" roared the mate. "Hard back on the oars!" They backed water desperately and just in time, for the vast tail rose thirty feet in the air and smashed down on the sea at the spot where they had been.

Macomber went charging forward and changed places with the big Negro.

"He's sounding!" the mate called aft. "Give him forty fathoms or so before you snub the line."

The slim manila rope was whirling out of the after tub now. Rod could hear it sing as it rounded the loggerhead and slithered forward between the rowers.

"Easy now," Macomber ordered. "Line's slacking off. He must be ready to surface again. Better snub."

Obediently Lucifer threw an extra loop over the sternpost. And no sooner had he done so than the boat took a sudden forward surge. Rod was jolted off the thwart and tumbled across the spare line-tub. As he regained his place he heard a terrified yell and felt the little craft tip dangerously, shipping water over the port gunwale.

"Man overboard!" someone cried. "It's Girty!"

"Let him go!" the mate replied. "Crazy fool—he jumped. Other boats'll pick him up. Hang on now—we're off for a sleighride!"

Clinging to the gunwale, Rod turned to look toward the bow. The whale was a full hundred yards ahead, swimming on the surface at tremendous speed, and spray was flying back in an arc on either side of the boat's sharp stem. They were being snatched through the water faster than the boy had ever traveled before.

Close above him, Lucifer held the steering oar in his big hands. The Negro's eyes rolled, showing the whites, and his lips moved constantly as if in prayer. Rod caught some of the words he was whispering and they sent a shiver down his spine.

"White!" breathed the giant hoarsely. "White as snow! Dat ain' no ord'nary black whale—mus' be ol' Dick, hisself!"

Something stirred in the boy's memory. It was that night in Boston when the bearded stranger in the chaise had taken him to supper. He remembered the grim lines of the man's face and the force of his words—"And if, in your wanderings, you should encounter that whale, may the Lord have mercy on your soul."

Time passed and still they sped on without slackening. The other boats were long since out of

sight, and only the topsails of the *Pelican* were
visible above the horizon.

"He's takin' us a thunderin' long way," one of
the seamen grumbled. "We're too fur now to be
seen from the ship. Hadn't we oughta cut, Mr.
Macomber?"

"No!" The mate's voice was harsh. "We're fast
to a hundred-barrel bull. He can't keep this up forever, an' when he's had enough we'll kill him."

There was silence after that. No talking. Only the
snarling rush of water along the strakes. To Rod
the boat seemed suddenly very small and frail and
lonely in that endless expanse of sea. And the
monster that had them in tow still showed no sign of
tiring. The boy wondered how far they had come.
Ten miles at least, he thought, in twice as many
minutes! If he lived, what a story this would be to
tell! Not even the oldest whaleman in the ship could
boast of such a ride.

At that moment the taut line went slack and the
flying craft lost way.

"Out oars," Macomber told them huskily. "The
critter won't sound now. He's used up too much air.
Here's our chance to get in on him."

But before they had straightened from the first
stroke, Lucifer gave a gasp and swung the long oar

powerfully to one side. "He's a-comin' fo' us, suh!" he yelled. "Watch out!"

Rod's eyes jerked sidewise and he was appalled at what he saw. The monster was swimming in a circle around the boat, his mighty flukes churning the water as he kept just beyond reach of the lance. Most of the enormous, hoary head showed above the waves, and the eye—hardly bigger than a man's—was fixed on them with a steady, baleful glare that made the boy's blood run cold.

"De white whale!" cried Lucifer in a strange, broken voice. "He's gwine kill us all!" And with that anguished scream he dropped the oar and leaped into the sea.

"Steer, Glenn!" the mate roared. "Bring us 'round!"

Rod sprang to the sweep handle and tried to force the boat's head about. With the other men pulling madly, he succeeded in making a half turn. Macomber poised the long lance. "Now—lay in—lay in!" he shouted.

It was too late. The whale's head lifted far above them and the long lower jaw dropped open, showing a double row of monstrous teeth. There was no time even to jump. With a splintering crash the jaw closed, chopping through oak keel and cedar planking—through flesh and blood and bone.

XIII

THE SHOCK of that awful moment numbed all Rod's faculties. How he escaped the fate of the others he never knew. All he could remember was swimming blindly, frantically, away from the horror he had seen. He was conscious of a tremendous commotion in the water behind him. Then gradually it subsided and he turned to look back, shaking the water out of his eyes. There was nothing there. No whale—no wreckage—no bobbing heads. Only the long, gray swells of the Pacific, rolling down out of the northeast.

All his boat-mates were gone. The big, kindly Quaker mate would never see his family in New Bedford again. Manuel, the Portuguese, was dead— and Lucifer and the others. It seemed a bitter thing that the cowardly Girty should be the only one alive besides himself.

Himself? How long could he expect to live, alone in that waste of ocean? The thought did not make him panicky. He weighed his chances coolly and knew how slight they were. But the will to survive was strong in him. Treading water, he bowed his head humbly and prayed that whatever lay ahead he might acquit himself like a man.

Then he put his mind on the grim problem of what could be done. The nearest land must be the island of Kauai, which they had sighted that morning. He tried to figure his present position and decided that the ship had been at least thirty miles northwest of the island when the boats were launched. But the whale's course, in that wild ride he had given them, was fairly close to due east. Rod could only guess at the distance they had been towed, but he was fairly sure that Kauai lay some twenty miles away to the southward. The idea gave him hope. It might be possible for a strong swimmer, aided by wind and current, to cover such a distance. He looked at the sun for his direction and started swimming—slowly and deliberately, so as not to waste his strength.

The two light garments he wore didn't hamper his movements, but he was conscious of the weight of the sheath knife at his belt. If he got rid of it now, it might mean the difference between reaching land and drowning. On the other hand, if sharks should come—he shivered. While he was trying to decide, his hand touched something solid and he recoiled in fright. Lifting his head he saw a tangle of wood and canvas floating a yard away. It was part of the boat's mast, sheered off by the whale's jaws, and with it were the boom and half of the triangular sail.

The spars were good pine, light and buoyant. Rod managed to cross the boom over the mast at right angles and pull the sail-cloth over them both. He had a sort of raft, not big enough to support his whole weight, but something he could lean on to ease his arms. That settled the question of the knife. He kept it.

Fortunately the water was fairly warm, and as long as the daylight lasted he felt no particular discomfort. Sometimes he floated and rested. More often he pushed the little raft before him and kicked steadily, trying to add something to the drift of the current. So far he had seen no sharks, and he did his best not to think of them.

After long hours the sun went down. One moment it was there, a red ball touching the rim of the sea on his right. Then he slid into the trough between two swells, and when he was lifted to the next crest there remained only a fiery glow in the west. Night began. In the darkness his courage ebbed away, and all his calculations about the direction of the island seemed like silly dreams. He was wet and tired and terribly alone.

Several times his exhaustion drugged him into sleep. Once the slipping of his hands from the mast wakened him. Thoroughly scared, he found a stray end of the sheet rope and tied it about him, so that whatever happened he would not lose his raft.

That night was like an eternity. Weakened by hunger and thirst and long exertion in the sea, he grew lightheaded in the hours before dawn. Sometimes it seemed to him that he was lost in a snowstorm, back in New Hampshire, or trying to reach the shore through a fog on Great Bay. Again he was trudging through dark, suffocating jungle, with Mahina Kea by his side. He could not see her face, but the touch of her hand was warm and comforting.

In his delirium he did not notice the first, faint lightening of the sky. It was only when the sun burst out of the ocean that he came back to full reality. His hands, shriveled by immersion in salt water, still clung instinctively to the butt of the mast. When he tried to loosen his grip the fingers, bent like birds' claws, refused to straighten. That struck him as somehow funny, and the sound of his own cackling laughter startled him.

Then he looked to the south and saw blue mountains with mist on their tops. He shook himself, rubbed his eyes and looked again. It was really there—a big island, looming high above the sea!

In his weakness, the miraculous sight made him weep like a baby. Then a flood of new energy ran through him. He kicked out strongly, forcing the raft toward shore, and sudden cramps seized him. His tortured leg muscles made him almost scream with pain. For five minutes he hung helpless on the broken mast, until his legs relaxed and the cramps left him. Whatever progress he made would have to come from wind and waves.

The island was perhaps five miles away when he first saw it, and for a long time it seemed to come no nearer. Then, in mid-forenoon, he realized he could see the white line of surf at the base of the cliffs.

Hours later, when the mountainous coast was barely two miles distant, he caught his first glimpse of a shark. The pointed gray dorsal fin cut lazily past him, then circled and came back on the other side. He struck the water with his arm several times and the fin veered off. Others appeared once or twice after that, but he succeeded in keeping them away. He thought of Moses Howland's words and knew how fortunate he had been in escaping the destruction of the boat without a wound. "Even a spoonful" of blood—and he would long since have been torn to pieces.

Gradually he became aware of a sound that was different from the wash of waves around him. It was the booming beat of breakers. A gull soared gracefully past, wheeled close to see if this bit of flotsam contained anything good to eat, and went on its landward course.

Rod had been in the water for more than twenty-four hours when he began to feel the tug of the surf. From close in, the coastline looked bleak and forbidding. For miles in either direction the dark cliffs rose straight out of the sea. Above them, opposite the spot where he was drifting, he saw green forest and a mighty rampart of mountain crags beyond. But there was no low land in sight—no beach on which he might hope to land.

The boy's heart sank. Had he come so near, only to be dashed to death on the rocks? He shut his eyes and clung to his spar, trusting in the Providence that had brought him through this desperate adventure still unscathed.

A big sea gathered under him and carried him forward with a thunderous rush. He felt his knee strike a jag of coral that must have been part of a submerged reef. Then he was dragged on, faster and faster. The wave broke over him with hammering force, burying his head under an avalanche of water. And as he struggled feebly to get back to the surface, his clawing fingers encountered sand. The next instant he was washed up, stunned and winded, on a narrow beach.

For a while he lay there, only half alive. Each breath he drew was an agony, and he had swallowed so much salt water that he was miserably sick. At last, when his stomach had emptied itself, he found the strength to crawl higher up the sloping sand. Black cliffs overhung the tiny stretch of beach. It was less than a hundred yards long, and the wall of rock crowded into the sea at either end. By some miracle he had been carried to the one bit of sand on all this cruel coast. With tears in his eyes he gave thanks for his deliverance.

In his drowsy weakness, Rod thought he heard a sound of little tinkling bells. It seemed to be somewhere behind him, and it came and went, often drowned out by the roar of the surf. Turning at last, he saw a silvery stream of water trickling down the sheer wall of the cliff. He got his feet under him and staggered to the bottom of the rocks. He thrust his face into the tiny waterfall, opened his parched lips and tasted the water. It was fresh and cold and wonderful. Eagerly he gulped down three or four mouthfuls and then his abused stomach rebelled. It was nearly an hour before he could really enjoy drinking.

The water brought back some of his strength. Looking about him he found the entrance of a low, shallow cave, a few yards from the stream. It was hardly more than a shelf hollowed out of the rock, at the eastern end of the beach, but its floor was above the tide line.

The boy went down to the edge of the sea and salvaged the mast, boom and frayed piece of sail that lay awash where he had left them. Hauling them up to the cave, he spread them there on the floor to dry. Then he returned to the surf. A few yards out he had seen a dark object like a human head bobbing in the spent breakers. Wading in, waist deep, he found a big coconut and carried it ashore.

The husk, he discovered with joy, was not water-logged. It must have fallen into the sea only a few hours before. Now he was grateful for the heavy sheath knife at his belt. Chopping awkwardly at first, he succeeded in cutting away the top of the husk and opening the green coconut inside. And never in all his life had any food tasted as good as the sweet milk it held.

Searching along the beach he found two more coconuts before darkness fell, and these he put away in the cave. For though he was still hungry he had no way of telling where his next meal was coming from.

The sun had set, and along this northern coast the light failed quickly. While he could still see, he crawled up into the cavern and lay down on the smooth stone. It was none too soon. Hardly had he made himself comfortable in his rocky shelter when a rain squall drenched the beach.

Lying there listening to the downpour outside, Rod took stock of his situation. For the moment, at least, he was alive and safe. But he had to face the fact that his chances of survival on that barren bit of sand were small indeed. There had been nothing about the wild, mountainous shore to suggest that people ever came there. About all he could hope for was that if he waited long enough a native canoe from some more habitable part of the island might pass within hailing distance. The only other way he could see to escape was to climb the cliffs and try to get over the *pali* itself. That would take far more energy than he had at present, but it might be done eventually if he could regain his full strength.

Soon the sound of the rain lulled him and his tired body relaxed. In spite of his hard bed, he slept like a log till daylight roused him.

The boy came awake with a jerk, reaching wildly for something to hold onto. The night and day he had spent in the ocean had left his nerves still shaky. As soon as he realized where he was he scrambled up, stretched his stiff muscles and peered out at the bright morning. The first thing his amazed eyes lit upon was what looked like a rounded, greenish-brown boulder moving slowly up the beach. Then he saw massive flippers and a scrawny neck, ending in a blunt head. It was a sea turtle, four feet long, waddling up the sand.

Rod crept out of the cave and approached the big turtle cautiously. It turned its head, blinked at him and crawled on, apparently unperturbed. On an impulse, the boy placed a bare foot on top of the dome-like shell, then stood erect, balancing while the huge beast carried him a yard or two. At last the turtle decided something was wrong. It craned its neck upward till it could see him, then pulled back its head and flippers as far inside the shell as they would go.

After his sleep Rod was tremendously hungry. He had no idea how raw turtle meat would taste, but it was food of a kind, and it was here for the taking.

He dismounted, lifted the side of the shell with all his strength, and succeeded in turning the two-hundred-pound creature over on its back. It sprawled there, pushing out its legs, trying vainly to right itself. Rod felt sorry for the helpless brute, but he was too famished to have any qualms about killing it. Quickly he thrust his knife into the leathery under-skin of the throat. Hardly had the turtle stopped kicking when he began to cut away the lower shell. And in a few minutes he was wolfing down pieces of the flesh.

It was rich meat, tough but not unpalatable. He knew that if he ate too much at this stage he might upset his stomach again, and he forced himself to stop after a few mouthfuls. Cutting away some good-sized chunks of meat, he wrapped it in wet seaweed and stored it away with his coconuts in the cave. Then, after a drink of water at the spring, he was ready to do some exploring.

XIV

IT HAD been close to high tide when Rod was washed ashore. Now, some sixteen hours later, the ebb was in progress. Tides here in the islands, he discovered, were less impressive than the ones he remembered on the New England coast. There was a variation of only three or four feet between ebb and flood. Where he stood, at the edge of the waves, he could see the scraps of weed and driftwood that marked the high-water line only a few yards away.

He looked over the debris on the beach with care, hoping to find something more in the way of food.

But there was little to interest him. No more coconuts had washed in during the night, and the only
remains of animal life were the bones of a small
fish and a dead crab. He went on to the western end
of the beach, then returned along the base of the
cliffs.

There was a narrow area above the tide line and
close to the rocks where a kind of coarse grass grew.
He gathered a few armfuls of it and carried them to
the cave. His piece of sail was fairly dry and he laid
it over the heap of grass to make a more comfortable
bed than the bare stone. Then he returned to give
the cliffs a closer scrutiny.

Search as he might, he could find no place that
would offer a hold for climbing. Once he succeeded
in getting six or seven feet up the face of the rock
only to be thwarted by an overhang it was impossible
to scale. The attempt kept him busy for several
minutes, and when he got to the ground again he
was startled to see a dozen more turtles, as big as the
one he had killed, sunning themselves on the beach.
As long as he could stomach raw turtle flesh it appeared that he wouldn't lack for food.

A swarm of crabs had attacked the carcass of the
dead reptile and were tearing fiercely at the bloody
shell and bones. Rod got the twelve-foot boom and
beat them off, then pushed the turtle down the sand

and into the water. There he hoped the crabs would finish off their job of scavenging before the body began to decompose.

As he carried the spar back to the cave he saw something that stopped him in his tracks. Hanging from the cliff, at the eastern angle where the beach ended, there was a long, snaky liana—the rope-like stem of some kind of vine. Its top was hidden by an outcropping shelf of the crag, forty feet above. The lower end swung gently in the morning breeze only two or three feet higher than his head.

Surely, the boy thought, no liana would be growing on that barren cliff. It was a tropical vine such as he had seen in the forest of the Nuuanu Valley. Somebody must have put it there—but who? It looked strong enough, but it might have been hanging from the rocks for years. The only way to find out was to test it for himself, and he was determined to make the attempt as soon as he had his strength back.

With that idea in mind, he went into the cave and ate some more turtle meat, then cut open another coconut and drank the milk. Well filled at last, he stretched out on the bed he had prepared. Rest, more than anything else, was what he needed now.

The months he had spent at sea had given Rod one useful habit. He could go to sleep almost the instant he lay down. The grass and canvas couch was at least as comfortable as a forecastle bunk, and as soon as he closed his eyes he dropped off into heavy slumber.

It was afternoon when a sound woke him. It was the rattling of a dislodged pebble. He opened his eyelids a crack and looked toward the cave mouth. There, outlined against the light, stood a human figure—a brown young Kanaka with a short spear in his hand!

"*Ala, haole,*" said the native youth. "Wake up, white man."

He came a cautious step nearer, holding his spear ready, and Rod sat up.

"*Aloha,*" he greeted the intruder, his tongue still thick with sleep.

For a moment neither of them knew just what to do next. The Hawaiian boy was still doubtful whether this young *haole* was a friend or an enemy, and Rod, realizing it, tried to appear harmless.

"*Aloha,*" he said again, and grinned broadly.

That seemed to do the trick. The native lad's stern face relaxed and he showed his teeth in a smile. He asked a question and Rod understood enough of what he said to answer after a fashion.

"*Waapa,*" he explained, using the word Smiling Jimmy had given him for "boat." He pointed out to sea, then to the broken mast and boom. *"Pau,"* he added, meaning "finished" or "done for."

The Hawaiian's face lighted up and he nodded. For a minute or two he talked rapidly but Rod was unable to catch more than a few words. He laughed and shook his head, holding up his hands. The other boy understood the gesture. He spoke more slowly.

"Owau," he said, pointing at his own breast, *"Kokua."* Then he pointed at Rod. *"Owai kou inoa?"* he asked.

The white boy grasped his meaning. He had told him his own name was Kokua and wanted to know Rod's.

In turn he pointed to himself. "Rod," he said, distinctly.

Kokua made several tries at the name but the nearest he could come to it was something that sounded like "Lok." There was no letter *R* or *D* in the Hawaiian alphabet. Finally he chuckled and went on to discuss other matters.

He wanted to know what the castaway had done for food—*"ai"*—and Rod showed him the turtle meat and the one remaining coconut. Their conversation went better now, for each used a sort of sign language to piece out the holes in Rod's vocabulary.

The Kanaka boy, as nearly as Rod could make

out, was from the other side of the island—the *kona*
or leeward side. He had climbed the *pali* on a hunt
for some kind of game and fallen from a cliff. He
showed the scar of a nearly healed bruise on one
of his thighs. He must have been in the jungle valley
at least two months, for he used the word *mahina*—
moon—and held up two fingers.

For food he had evidently found an old taro plant-
ing. He repeated the word *poi* more than once, and
worked his arms as if he were pounding something
in a depression of the rock. Also he conveyed the
information that plenty of coconut palms grew on
the slopes above the first line of cliffs. He had seen
turtles on the beach from up there, and had rigged
the liana as a means of getting down to them.

Rod tried to find out if parties of Kanakas ever
visited this coast. It was a difficult question to phrase,
and it took Kokua some time to understand it.
Finally he got the idea and shook his head. He had
not seen a single boat during his weeks in the valley.
Then he shrugged his shoulders expressively and
grinned. From some of the words he used, and the
way he pointed to his smooth, well-filled belly, Rod
gathered that he wasn't too worried about being
rescued.

He went to the mouth of the cave now and
beckoned for the white boy to follow him. As he

stood there in the afternoon light, naked except for his loincloth of woven leaves, he was the picture of a young island warrior, brown, graceful and smooth-muscled. Rod looked down at his own garb and laughed. The tatters of his dungarees hung scarecrow-like around his lean legs. His shirt had simply disappeared during his battle with the sea, and his scratched, sun-burned ribs stuck out like the ridges on a washboard.

"Hele mai," said Kokua. "Come." And he pointed to the hanging end of the liana.

"Don't know if I can make it," Rod told him, "but I'll do my best. Hold on, though—how about some *ai?"*

He went back into the cave and brought out the bundle of meat and the green coconut. Kokua sniffed at the turtle flesh and found it fresh enough. But he tossed the coconut aside disdainfully. Pointing to the top of the cliff he gestured widely with his hands to indicate that plenty of *niu* grew up there.

In a moment the young Kanaka had torn a strip of canvas from the tattered edge of the sail, wrapped the meat in it and tied the two ends about his waist. Then, jumping upward, he caught the liana and began climbing hand over hand.

Rod watched, envious of the boy's agile strength. He saw how Kokua made the ascent easier by grip-

ping the vine with his ankles or the soles of his bare
feet. After a minute or two he disappeared over a
ledge, forty feet above, but Rod could hear him
calling—*"Hele mai—hele mai!"*

The New England lad pulled his belt tight and
drew a deep breath. Measuring the distance he
leaped as high as he could and his hands clutched
the ropelike liana. A month earlier it would have
been an easy climb for the young sailor. Now, weak
from his ordeal in the sea, he had to put forth all
his strength to haul himself up. At last he was high
enough to hold the rough liana between his knees
and could lift himself with both arms instead of one
at a time.

The vine seemed to stretch endlessly above him
but he kept on climbing resolutely and never looked
down. When he reached the edge of the rock shelf,
Kokua was there to give him a hand. Panting and
exhausted he was dragged up to the safety of the
ledge.

Rod recovered his breath and looked about him.
They appeared to be at least half way up the cliff, for
he could see palm fronds overhanging the rocks,
thirty feet above. Kokua grinned encouragingly and
went up the liana like a monkey. This time the cliff
face sloped back a little and it was possible to "walk"
upward with feet braced against the stone. As soon

as the Hawaiian boy reached the top, Rod followed him. And a moment later they stood together on the grassy crest.

Kokua faced inland and threw out his arm in a sweeping gesture. *"Kalalau,"* he said simply.

They were on the seaward edge of a great green valley, miles in length, that seemed to have been cut out of the island's mountainous backbone. On three sides, east and south and west, it was walled in by gigantic cliffs. They stretched upward for thousands of feet, their tops half hidden by drifting mists. Borne by the trade wind, small showers of rain chased areas of brilliant sunshine across the sloping valley floor. The thick jungle was alternately dark and vivid green, and high on the eastern rim was such a rainbow as Rod had never seen.

The beauty of the place took his breath away. "Kalalau," he repeated in a whisper. It was a name he would remember as long as he lived.

Kokua was proud of his valley and happy to watch the white boy's reaction. But after a few minutes he beckoned Rod to follow him and led the way up a faintly marked path among the ferns and coconut palms. Half a mile up the slope they came out on a small grassy plateau. At one side was a broken-down retaining wall of stones that looked as if they had been there a long time. Kokua pointed to the tops of taro plants, growing in a straggly row above the wall.

"Kalo," he said. *"Poi."* He crossed the little meadow to a grass-roofed shack at the edge of the forest. Evidently he had built it himself out of tree branches, for he showed his handiwork with considerable pride. By the doorway there was a fire-pit for cooking and a roughly hollowed stone with a smaller, egg-shaped stone on top. It was a crude version of the mortar and pestle used by the islanders to pound taro root and make *poi.*

Going to a corner of the hut, Kokua reached under a mat of green leaves and pulled out a good-sized calabash. It was filled with the grayish-white paste that Rod remembered from the *hukilau.*

"Hele mai ai!" Kokua said. "Come and eat!"

He thrust his fingers into the gourd and pulled them out dripping with *poi,* which he devoured noisily and with gusto. At his invitation, Rod followed suit. The stuff was slightly fermented and had a tangy, sourish taste that he began to like after the first mouthful. It went down smoothly and he kept on eating till the calabash was empty. *Poi,* he decided, must be an amazing food. He felt not only well filled but twice as strong as when he left the beach.

There were still two or three hours of daylight

left. Kokua gathered some dry ferns and grass, then some bark and sticks. From a sort of pocket in the fold of his loincloth he carefully drew out a flint-stone and a small piece of steel. Holding them close to the heap of tinder on the ground, he struck one against the other patiently, until a spark caught the dry leaves and flared into a tiny flame.

He motioned to Rod to fetch more wood while he nursed the fire. Over among the trees the white boy found some dead branches which he dragged back to the shack. He broke them into short lengths and piled them at Kokua's side.

When the blaze had burned long enough to form a sizable pile of red coals, the young Kanaka pushed them into the fire-hole, covered them with a layer of green leaves and put the turtle meat on top. This, in turn, was covered with more leaves and a few inches of earth filled the pit up to ground level. The simple contraption was not unlike the "bean-holes" in which New Englanders had baked their beans for generations.

The cooking, Rod knew, would be a slow process, probably lasting all night. Meanwhile Kokua had other activities in mind. He led the white boy back into the forest and pointed out various trees, naming them as they went along. Evidently he meant to educate Rod whether he wanted it or not. There were big *koa* and *kohala* trees; *hau* trees with long, curving branches; *kukui* trees, which bore a kind of nut; and here and there a breadfruit tree, called *ulu* in Hawaiian.

Rod had an armful of fruit and nuts when they returned. Kokua carried a good-sized bundle of *lauhala,* the long leaves of the pandanus. While the white boy amused himself by sampling the various edibles, his new-found companion split the leaves into shreds and hung them on a stick to dry for weaving.

At sunset they went down the hill to the palm grove along the edge of the cliff. Kokua selected a tree with a slanting trunk and ran up it like a cat. At the top he picked three or four green coconuts and tossed them down to Rod. They cut off the tops and drank their fill of coconut milk, then made their way back to the shack.

Deep shadows had fallen over the valley now, and it would soon be night. Kokua spread out a *lauhala* mat inside the hut. There was room for only one person to lie on it, but he insisted that it was for Rod. *"Hoi e moe,"* he urged. "Go to bed." He brought an armful of ferns for his own couch and lay down in the other corner of the hut. In a few moments they were both asleep.

XV

ROD MUST have slept a full twelve hours. A beam of sunlight coming over the eastern cliffs, entered the doorway of the hut and shone directly in his eyes. He blinked, yawned and sat up, stretching the kinks out of his muscles. Then he looked about for Kokua. His young host had evidently risen earlier, for he could hear him moving around outside.

"Aloha kakahiaka!" the Kanaka boy greeted him as he appeared at the entrance. "Good morning!"

He was holding a big calabash filled with water, and he offered it to Rod with a grin.

He drank gratefully. In his limping Hawaiian he asked where the water came from, and Kokua showed him a spring near the edge of the jungle. Surely, Rod thought, this valley of Kalalau provided everything a castaway could ask.

Kokua had built a fresh fire and was heating stones to cook breadfruit and taro. Meanwhile he brought out another gourd of *poi* from his leafy cupboard and they ate it for breakfast.

Suddenly the sharp-eyed Hawaiian touched Rod's arm and pointed up the valley. On an outcrop of rock, a mile away above the jungle, the white boy saw a moving gray speck. It was a four-footed animal—a goat, he thought.

Kokua's eyes gleamed. "Come on," he said in Kanaka. "Let's go on a hunt."

He took his spear, made of a long, sharpened stone bound with thongs to a four-foot wooden shaft, and they started into the forest.

Rod had all he could do to keep up with the native boy. It was mostly uphill going, and Kokua moved at a half trot, climbing over rocks, skirting vine-choked thickets, squirming through masses of tall, rank fern. He seemed to know every turn and short cut like the palm of his own hand.

The young whaler was panting and wet with perspiration when they neared the spot where the goat had been seen. Kokua waited for him and held up a warning hand. *"Kulikuli,"* he whispered. "Keep quiet."

He crept along to the foot of a pile of broken rock, parted the leaves with his hands and peered upward. The animal must still be in sight, for Kokua's grin was excited as he tiptoed back. In silent pantomime he showed Rod what he wanted him to do. The Kanaka boy would make a circuit to the other side of the rocky hill and climb up there. Rod was to wait a short time, then go up the boulders on the near side, driving the game in Kokua's direction.

For five minutes after Kokua departed, Rod crouched in the undergrowth. When he figured enough time had passed he pushed forward silently and looked up at the crag. The goat was feeding on some sparse grass that grew in a niche on the side of the rocks. It was a big beast, long-legged and active-looking, and it had a pair of sweeping horns that would measure a yard from tip to tip.

Still moving quietly, the boy began to climb. The tumbled boulders made a series of giant steps up which he scrambled. The breeze was blowing from him toward the goat, and before he had advanced far the animal heard him or caught his scent. It swung its head from side to side, then gave an agile leap and vanished around a rocky corner of the hill.

Rod kept on climbing. Just as he reached the place where the goat had been feeding, he heard a savage yell from Kokua. He shouted encouragement and ran up the rough hillside as fast as he could go, and as he rounded a rocky shoulder he almost collided head-on with the goat. The surprise of this meeting stopped them both in their tracks. For an instant Rod didn't know what to do, for the ledge on which they stood was only two or three feet wide. If the animal charged him he would certainly be pitched down to the rocks below. For the goat there was no such indecision. It sprang lightly out into space, landed for a fraction of a second on a tuft of grass part way down the cliff, then twisted sidewise and went bounding off along the lower ledges.

With a helpless feeling, Rod watched their quarry escape. But he had underestimated his companion's skill as a hunter. He saw Kokua jump out of a cranny in the rocks just as the goat passed and dart his spear into its side behind the shoulder. The beast ran on half a dozen yards, then stumbled and lay kicking and thrashing.

It was still alive and putting up a battle when Rod scrambled down to his friend's side. Kokua was gripping the horns with both hands.

"Pahi!" he gasped. "The knife!"

Rod whipped out his blade and quickly put an end to the wounded creature's struggles. The two boys rested a few minutes, looking over their kill with pride. It was an old male, wiry and probably tough, but it was fresh meat. Kokua's spear had missed the heart and pierced one of the lungs.

They cut away the haunches and loins, leaving the rest of the carcass to the buzzards which were already wheeling in circles overhead. And well loaded with meat, the young hunters went down the trail to Kokua's camp once more.

*   *   *

Time had no special meaning in that wild and lovely valley. Rod lost track of the passage of days. There were sunrises and sunsets, rain showers and golden afternoons. It was never too cold, and the sun's heat was always tempered by breezes off the sea.

They did not lack for food or for things to do. A few days of eating *poi,* goat's flesh, turtle meat, breadfruit and coconuts put the solid muscle back on Rod's bones. Meanwhile they were busy hunting, exploring, cooking and making things to wear or use.

Under Kokua's patient teaching Rod wove him-

self a *malo,* or loincloth, out of the long shreds of
lauhala leaves. It was finished in time to replace
his ragged dungarees before they fell apart in tatters.
He also fashioned himself a spear. It took two days
of careful chipping to sharpen a flintstone to the
proper shape and keenness. A stick of seasoned iron-
wood made the shaft, and they used tough goat
sinews to bind the head and shaft together. He never
learned to use the spear as expertly as Kokua, but
even in his hands it was a formidable weapon.

A few days after the spear was completed they
went far up the valley on another hunt. By this time
Rod had made real progress with the Hawaiian
language, and they were able to talk almost as easily
as if the Kanaka boy had been an American.

Kokua told him he was hungry for pork, and there
was a good chance that they might find wild pig on
the high benches near the head of the valley. He
warned him, however, that the wild pigs of Kauai
were nothing to trifle with. The full-grown males
were big, rangy and fierce, and they had curving
tusks—he illustrated with his fingers—that could
rip a man open like a split coconut husk.

Half an hour's climbing brought them out of the
rank jungle of the lower valley into a parklike
country of Hawaiian pine and hardwood. There
were open glades among the trees, and under foot lay

pine cones, nuts and acorns—good forage for pig, as Kokua pointed out.

In the mud of a stream gulley they found fresh tracks, where many pigs appeared to have wallowed within the past few hours. Kokua picked up the trail and moved quickly along, his sharp eyes scanning the ground as he went. Perhaps because he was so preoccupied, it was Rod who first sighted the herd of porkers.

"Look!" he whispered. "Over there under the trees!"

There were at least half a dozen of the animals— a big, black boar, two sows and several young shoats. They were rooting for nuts, still unaware of danger.

The two boys crouched behind a lantana bush and planned their strategy. Kokua said he would try to make a circuit and get on the other side. Then, whichever way they ran, there might be a chance to strike one. "Go for the little pigs," he told Rod. "They're better eating and they can't move as fast as the old ones."

Kokua crawled off through the brush and Rod waited, gripping his spear. But something went wrong with the plan. Whether the Kanaka boy made a noise or whether the wind brought them his scent, Rod didn't know. He saw the big tusker raise its head suspiciously, then snort and gallop away with the others following.

One of the smaller pigs fell behind and the boy thought he saw an opportunity to catch it. He raced after the herd, exultant to find himself gaining rapidly on the straggler.

"Kokua!" he shouted. *"Hele mai—wikiwiki!* Come here, quick!"

He was almost on top of the young pig now, but the elusive beast dodged back and forth, offering a poor target. Twice Rod lunged with his spear without touching the shoat. Then, by a lucky stroke, he stabbed it in the haunch just above the hock and hamstrung it. The pig let out a plaintive squeal and hobbled a few steps on three legs, but it was no longer able to dodge. Dropping his spear, the boy drew his knife and flung himself on the unfortunate animal. He had driven the blade deep into the pig's throat when he heard a warning cry behind him.

"Run!" yelled Kokua. "It's the big one!"

Glancing up in haste, Rod saw the boar charging in like a black whirlwind. Its little eyes were red with fury and its curling tusks dripped foam.

The terrified boy had only seconds in which to act. As he scrambled to his feet he saw a tree limb a yard above his head. With a desperate leap he caught it and dragged himself up, swinging his legs high to

grip the branch. For the moment at least he was safe.

Below his perch the enraged boar jumped upward in a vain attempt to reach him. Failing in this, the brute rushed at the trunk of the tree and tore at the bark with its scimitar-like teeth. And during that moment Kokua had his chance. The young Kanaka came up on the boar's left side, measured the distance coolly, and drove home the spear with all the power of his arm and shoulder. The blade went in deep and true. With a hoarse grunt of pain the big beast slumped forward and died, pierced through the heart.

Kokua, panting but happy, sat beside his kill while Rod climbed down and recovered his knife and spear. "You did well," the Kanaka boy said. "The small pig will be tender and sweet. I was afraid the big one would catch you, but you were too quick for him."

The meat on the boar was so tough and stringy that they abandoned the body after a few attempts to cut it. However, Kokua broke the tusks out of the skull with a rock and saved them for ornaments. The younger pig was fat and well-fed. They tied its feet together and slung it on a pole that could be carried between them on their shoulders. It weighed about a hundred pounds, Rod thought, but that was when they first picked it up. Long before they got back to the shack he had decided that the pig was a good deal heavier.

They cleaned the carcass, stuffed it with breadfruit and roasted it whole in a pit Kokua dug with his hands. Rod meanwhile had gone down to the beach and collected a handful of precious salt, sun-dried from sea water on a hollowed stone. With the salt for seasoning, the roast pork was as delicious as any meat he had ever tasted.

There were other hunts, but none more thrilling or more successful than that one. As week after week went by, Rod's body hardened and his skin grew so brown that Kokua was only a shade or two darker than he. He was thriving on the food he ate. In all his life he had never felt better. But there was not enough work to use up all his energies. Restless, he went off sometimes by himself, ranging far up the valley and along the wall of cliffs. It was on one of these excursions that he ran into a strange experience.

Like many Hawaiians, Kokua was an easy-going kind of person. Unless there was something that really needed doing he was content to loaf in the sunshine, and he laughed at Rod's unwillingness to sit still. On this particular day their larder was well supplied with food and all their equipment was in good shape. After pulling a few weeds in the taro patch, Kokua stretched out comfortably on the grass and took a nap. The New England boy wandered about impatiently for a while, then took his spear and set out toward the windward cliffs that walled the valley on the eastern side.

He followed no trail but beat his way through the jungle, watching the bright-plumaged birds flitting ahead of him among the trees. After walking perhaps half a mile he found himself close under the shadowy crags. A cloud passed over the sun and a sharp little shower drenched him with chilling rain. The wind that swept down the cliffs made an eerie, wailing sound. He shivered without quite knowing why.

For a moment Rod paused. He had no particular purpose in going farther, and there was something menacing about that wall of rock that reached up and up till it was lost in the dark mists. Then he shook himself, angry at his own hesitation. Striding forward, he began to climb the broken rubble that lay along the cliff's base.

Soon he was high enough to look back over the treetops. He could even see the little meadow where Kokua's hut stood, and a wisp of blue smoke wavering above it. The Kanaka boy must have roused himself and started a cook-fire. Turning back to

continue his climb, Rod noticed something odd
about the rocks just above him. Instead of a jumble
of broken stone scattered on the slope, these were
rounded boulders, each about the size of a small
barrel. Laid in a fairly even row, they formed a wall
about a dozen yards in length.

As he got closer he could see that they had been
there a long, long time. There was moss on their
sides, and plants had taken root in the crevices between them. Rod's curiosity was stirred. He found a
foothold below the line of stones and hauled himself
up till he could look over them. The side of the
cliff was much closer than he had realized. It
loomed starkly upward only a few feet away. And
there in the smooth wall of rock he saw a cave. Its
entrance was not very high or wide but it appeared
to reach far back into the cliff. The daylight
penetrated only a short distance. Beyond, it was
black as midnight.

XVI

THERE was a feeling in the air of the place that was gloomy and foreboding. Rod started toward the cave, then drew back, gripped by an instinct close to fear. Again he examined the row of boulders, wondering whose hands had placed them there so long ago. The narrow space between the stones and the cave mouth was level and grass-grown, quite different from the rest of the rocky scarp. Like the wall, it must have been the work of men.

"Well," the boy told himself, "there's nothing

here to be afraid of. What am I waiting for?" He turned to enter the cave but stopped when he saw a rough carving on the stone beside it. Lines representing two figures, much like the matchstick people that children draw, had been crudely cut into the face of the rock. One of the pictured men lay flat, as if stretched on the ground. The other stood over him with a weapon of some kind in his hand. Obviously the carving was meant to tell the story of a fight in which one contestant had been killed.

Once more Rod mustered up his courage and walked boldly into the low, black cavern. After three or four steps he had to grope his way with outstretched hands. In the pitch darkness, moisture dripped down from the dank stone and he could hear the muffled echo of his own breathing.

Then there was a sudden rushing sound. A big black shape brushed past his face, so close that the wind of its going ruffled his hair. Scared and shaken, he swung about and beat a hasty retreat. Even though common sense told him the thing that had passed him was only a bat, he had no stomach for further exploration at that moment.

Rod had no difficulty finding his way back to the hut, for trampled ferns and broken bushes marked the way he had come. Kokua was squatting on his

heels beside the hollowed *poi* rock, pounding cooked
taro root with a big round stone.

"Where did you go?" he asked the white boy.
"There is trouble on your face. You must have seen
something evil."

Rod grinned sheepishly. "Nothing very bad," he
replied. "Just an old cave in the side of the mountain. But for a minute I guess I was *maka'u*—
afraid."

He told Kokua about the wall of stones and the
carving at the entrance. "It was too dark to see anything inside," he concluded. "Then some kind of bat
or bird came flying past my face and—well—I left."

The Kanaka nodded. "What you found was a
burial place," he said. "I, too, have been frightened
when I was in the abode of the dead. This man—a
chief, perhaps—must have died very long ago.
There have been no people in this valley since before my father's memory."

He went back to his taro pounding, holding the
stone in both hands. After a moment he looked up
again and grinned.

"So that you may be no longer afraid," he said,
"I will go with you tomorrow to the cave. With
torches we can see what is inside."

They spent part of the afternoon gathering ripe
coconuts and squeezing oil out of the hard, rancid

meat. When they had a cup of it, Kokua showed Rod how to twist a handful of long grass into a compact sheaf, and tie it with tough leaf stems. They prepared half a dozen of these torches and tried one of them that night to see how it worked. Dipped in coconut oil, the grass burned evenly for two or three minutes. It gave about as much light as a tallow candle, Rod thought.

As they sat there watching the flame flicker and die, Kokua told his companion more about the tombs of island warriors. "In the old days," he said, "before the missionaries came, it was forbidden to go near such a burial place. If one of our people broke the *kapu* he was put to death. A chief who died in battle had the right to lie in peace, with his war club and spear, and a little food for his long journey.

"There were strange, bad customs in those times. For a woman or girl to eat in the presence of any man was *kapu*. She was killed or had her eyes burned out. And when a king or a high chief died, all children ran and hid in the forest. They knew the priests would put young boys and girls to the knife, to satisfy their cruel gods with blood."

Kokua's face was somber as he told these things. Rod shivered. Looking up at the tropic stars above the black jungle, he could almost feel the presence of ancient, savage spirits, lurking near them in the shadows. He would hardly have been surprised if he had heard the throb of war drums or seen the ghost of a long-dead warrior.

Troubled by these imaginings, he did not sleep very well that night. The sound of Kokua's voice, raised in a cheerful Hawaiian song, woke him at sunrise, and looking out at the golden light of morning he forgot all about his friend's gruesome tales.

They breakfasted and made ready to visit the burial cave. Kokua carried the oil, which he had poured into a coconut shell so that it wouldn't spill. Rod had the twists of grass and each of them took his spear as a matter of course.

The Kanaka boy led the way, following Rod's trail as easily as if it had been a village street. "You leave a wider track than a herd of wild pigs," he chuckled. "If we had enemies in this valley, they would find us quickly."

He broke through the foliage at the foot of the scarp and paused, just as Rod had done, staring up at the towering height of the cliffs.

"Look up there." Rod pointed. "See the old wall?"

Kokua nodded. "Many times I have hunted this side of the valley," he said, "but never at this place.

It is as you say. The stones were put there by the hands of men."

They climbed up over the rubble and stood on the grassy shelf before the cave. Kokua studied the carving on the stone for some moments.

"Ae," he said finally. "Yes, it is old—perhaps fifty years—perhaps more. Both these warriors were chiefs, but the one who was slain was not of the Kauai people. The mark of a stranger is cut here in the stone beside his head. He came from a far-off island. But though he was killed, his warriors must have won the battle or they would have had no chance to bury their leader here."

Rod was impressed by the boy's clever reasoning and told him so. Kokua merely shrugged. "Such picture-writing as this," he said, "is meant to be read. It is like the books at the missionary school—only easier. Come—get the torches ready and we will go in."

At that moment a rain cloud darkened the sky above them and swirling mists came down the face of the cliff. If Rod had been alone he might have been tempted to turn back, for once more he felt that chill of foreboding he had experienced the day before. But Kokua paid no attention to the sudden gloom. Under the shelter of the cave mouth he dipped a torch in his oil-filled shell and proceeded to strike a spark with flint and steel. When the grass taper was burning he led the way confidently into the cavern.

The black passage widened abruptly after they had gone a dozen steps. Along the ledges of the walls they could see bats hanging by their wing hooks— dark, velvety blotches against the stone. Disturbed by the light, several of the creatures detached themselves and came sweeping by with a rush that nearly put out the flame.

"Hele iwaho oe!" the Kanaka boy grunted angrily. "Get out, you!"

He shielded the flickering light with his hand and went on more cautiously. Following close behind, Rod could see nothing of what lay in front of them. He almost trod on Kokua's bare heels when the young Hawaiian came to a sudden halt.

"Here it is," the boy said quietly. "The chief sleeps well in his canoe."

Rod stepped to one side and looked where Kokua pointed. The little light gleamed on dark, polished wood, and he could see the outlines of a long dugout canoe, placed in the center of the cave.

The first torch was about to burn itself out, and they lighted another. Then, side by side, they tiptoed forward to look into the narrow boat that served as a coffin. The bones of a skeleton lay white and stark in the bottom of the canoe. Gathered about the shoulders and reaching down along the sides was a feather cape, bright with yellows, reds and greens. A long, heavy spear with a stone tip lay clasped in the warrior's right hand.

"A big man," Kokua whispered. "Tall, and strong-boned. I told you he was a great chief. Look at the cape. Not even the kings wore handsomer feathers than these. He has a fine canoe, too, made differently from ours."

He tapped the shell of the dugout and it gave off a ringing sound that echoed loudly in the cavern.

"The wood is still solid," Kokua said. "Thin and light but very strong. No Kanaka of Kauai has seen such a canoe in my lifetime. It must have come from Oahu or even from the Big Island."

The same idea must have struck both the boys at that instant, for they stared at each other without speaking. Rod was the first to break silence.

"Solid!" he said. "You mean—it would float?"

He lighted a fresh torch, while Kokua knelt down, searching along the craft's under side with his fingers. When he stood up, there was powdery brown dust on his palm, and he frowned.

"Dry rot!" the white boy exclaimed in disappointment. "Gee—I thought for a minute we had a boat."

"Perhaps we have," Kokua answered. "But we must take it outside before we know."

He turned a sober face toward the skeleton in the canoe and spoke in a kind of chanting sing-song. "Forgive us, warrior from another island," he said. "If we break your long rest, it is because we have no boat and are far from home."

Gently he began lifting out the bones and laying them on the cave floor. Rod helped him and they re-arranged the skeleton as best they could, careful that each bone should occupy its proper place.

As Kokua set the head in position, he pointed to a broken area above the eye, where the skull was crushed inward. "A war club did that," he said. "Or it may have been a stone from a sling."

As Rod put the spear down by the dead chief's side the last of their grass tapers burned out. But by now their eyes were used to the darkness. A faint light entered from the mouth of the cavern, and they could still make out the shape of the canoe.

"It would be easier to carry if it had outriggers," Kokua said. "But it may not be too heavy. You take the forward end and I will stay back here. Shall we try it?"

Rod found the bow an awkward thing to take hold of. The canoe was only twenty inches wide, but its straight sides were nearly two and a half feet high. He fumbled for a moment, trying to get a grip around the smooth surface. Then, feeling inside the prow, his fingers came on a narrow cavity, hollowed out of the wood. It was just big enough to serve as a handhold and had certainly been put there for that purpose.

He slipped the four fingers of his right hand into the hole and lifted. At the second try the bow came off the stone floor. "All right," he told Kokua. "Say when you're ready."

The Kanaka boy had been able to get his arms around the stern. "Now," he panted. "Both together."

They raised the hundred-and-fifty-pound craft and carried it slowly toward the cave entrance. With a sigh of relief Rod set his end down on the grassy *lanai* and straightened his aching fingers. He looked at the half mile of jungle that separated them from Kokua's clearing and wondered if they had bitten off more than they could chew.

The Kanaka boy must have had the same thought, for Rod saw a wry grin on his face as he stretched his arm muscles.

The shower had gone by and the wet grass sparkled in the sunlight. Carefully Kokua took the feather cape from the canoe and draped it over a rock, where its colors glowed like many-colored jewels. Then he heaved the dugout over on its side, exposing the bottom.

There were several places where the hull had rotted away to half an inch or more in depth. However, when Rod scraped away the loose particles they found the wood sound underneath. They tapped on it, inside and out, and decided it was still watertight except for one long crack, half way up the starboard side. Rod thought that this could be calked, and after he had explained what he meant in sign language, Kokua nodded agreement. Coconut fiber would do, he said. It was what the natives used to patch old boats.

As the white boy stood up he saw a small leather bag, tied with a thong, that must have fallen out of the canoe when it was tipped over. He picked it up. "What do you suppose this is?" he asked, shaking the pouch. It felt light but something rattled inside.

"Food for the dead man's journey," Kokua replied carelessly. "Nuts or fruit. It must have dried away in all these years."

Rod started to throw the object away, but on second thought he tied the end of the thong to his belt. He might find a use for the little bag some day.

"Well," he said, "how are we going to get our boat over to the camp and down to the beach?"

"Part of the way we can carry it," said the

Kanaka. "Part of the way we can roll it on round logs. But all this will take days. The canoe will be safe enough here, but before the rain comes again I want to put this cape under the thatch of my hut. Also," he grinned, "I am hungry."

He smoothed the lovely feather-work with his hands and folded the cape inside out so that it would come to no harm on the way through the jungle. "If I ever reach Hanapepe again," he told Rod, "this will make me a famous man. People will walk far to see and touch it. And when I wear it, on feast days, strangers will say, 'Look—surely he is the son of a great chief!'"

They lunched on *poi* and coconut milk and Kokua put hot coals in the *imu*—the oven-pit—to roast goat's meat and breadfruit for their evening meal.

"When we have rested," he said, "we will find a dead tree the size of a fat man's thigh, and build fires under the trunk to cut it in pieces. With two or three such rollers to put under the canoe we can save our backs."

Rod wasn't listening. A moment before he had remembered the little leather pouch at his waist, untied the thong and opened it. Now he sat staring, openmouthed, at what he had found inside. There in the palm of his hand lay a dozen huge, gleaming pearls, and the bag contained many more!

XVII

ROD KNEW what they were. Once, in a jeweler's window at Portsmouth, he had seen a pair of pearl earrings valued at a hundred dollars. These were twice as large. They were big as cranberries and perfect in their rounded smoothness. They glowed softly in his hand, their milky white color shot through with iridescent tints of blue and green and pink.

Kokua came closer and touched the jewels with his finger. He seemed more curious than impressed.

"I have seen such beads before," he volunteered.

"Fishermen get them from oyster shells. They make *leis* of them to go around the necks of chiefs' wives, but ginger flowers are prettier and have a sweeter smell."

Rod brought the *lauhala* mat from the shack and carefully spread the pearls out on it. There were thirty of them, all of the same size and luster.

"Here," he told the Kanaka boy. "Half of these are yours."

Kokua laughed. "No," he said. "If you like them, keep them. I have the feather cape, which is much finer."

Rod replaced the pearls in the leather bag and tied it securely to his belt. Perhaps Kokua's idea of values was more sensible than his own. Certainly as long as they stayed in this lost valley, the gems were a handful of useless "beads" and nothing more.

They found a fallen tree of the right size not far from the clearing. Kokua built a series of fires under the trunk, four or five feet apart, and Rod was kept busy the rest of the afternoon foraging for dry sticks to feed the flames. By sundown the last of the sections was burned through. They carried the rollers back to camp, ate their evening meal and went to bed, planning an early start and a big day's work next day.

When they set out for the cave in the early morning, each of them carried two of the round logs. Kokua soon pointed out, however, that they would have to cut some sort of trail if they wanted to move the canoe, so they left the rollers at the edge of the clearing and began hacking a path through the jungle. It was hot, heavy work. Rod dulled the edge of his knife, chopping through tough vines and bushes. He had to whet it on a flat stone several times before they had covered half the distance.

By midafternoon they were both so tired that they hardly cared whether they got the canoe out or not. Kokua gave up when they came to a particularly dense thicket. He went back to camp to prepare supper while Rod labored on alone till dusk.

He made his way back, sore and discouraged and more than a little disgusted at his friend for quitting. But it was impossible to stay angry at the young Kanaka for very long. He was as good-natured and irresponsible as a puppy where hard work was concerned. At least he was a good cook, and the meal of breadfruit and *poi* put new heart in Rod.

They tackled the job again next morning and by noon a twisting but fairly serviceable trail was completed all the way to the foot of the cliff. The frequent showers that fell on that side of the valley had left several inches of water in the bottom of the canoe. They tipped it out and succeeded in getting their awkward load over the retaining wall and down to the foot of the scarp.

Now the rollers were brought into play. They worked fairly well where the ground was smooth, but it was a slow business at best. Any unevenness would catch the round logs and wedge them fast, so that the boys had to slide the dugout along or lift it over. In the end they carried the canoe many more yards than they rolled it.

Rod had difficulty in keeping Kokua interested in the tiresome task. The Hawaiian boy saw no need to hurry. He pointed out that they were well enough off in their valley. It made little difference whether they got the canoe out now or a month from now. The young Yankee had different ideas. He had started a job and he meant to stick to it until he finished.

When Kokua wanted to take a nap or go hunting, Rod kept him at work by telling him stories. He described bleak New England winters, the deep-drifted snow and the roaring log fires. He told about skating on frozen ponds, but this was almost more than the Kanaka boy could believe. Water that became hard as a stone in the cold was beyond his comprehension.

Rod's whaling adventures were more easily understood. Kokua had seen whales and whale-boats, and the harpoon was first cousin to a Hawaiian fish spear. He listened over and over again to the story of the fight with the white whale, his dark eyes gleaming with excitement.

After three days of straining and struggling, they carried the canoe out of the jungle and set it down near the shack. Kokua celebrated by preparing the first real feast they had eaten in nearly a week. He went down to the beach and killed a turtle, opened half a dozen coconuts and got out a calabash full of prime *poi*. When the turtle meat was cooked, they ate till they could hold no more and rested till bedtime.

"Tomorrow," said Kokua, "we will get *hau* branches and start making our outrigger."

In the morning he led the way into the forest and showed Rod the kind of limbs they needed. The main beam should be about five inches through and slightly curved, he explained. The cross-braces could be somewhat smaller—about the thickness of his arm, and eight or ten feet long. If possible, they must find dead limbs, light and dry but thoroughly sound.

Fortunately nearly all branches on a *hau* tree have a natural curve, and within an hour the boys had located dead limbs of the right size. They brought them back to the clearing and Rod trimmed them to the proper lengths with his sheath knife.

The hull of the dugout already had holes bored in its sides near the top to hold the outrigger lashings. Kokua brought in long strips of palm fiber which they braided into tough, three-strand cords, five or six feet long. When they had made half a dozen of these ropes they were ready to put the outrigger in place. First the cross-braces were laid across the canoe, with one end of each extending about six feet out on the port side. The curve in the wood brought the outer ends nearly down to ground level. Kokua now lashed each brace solidly to both gunwales of the canoe.

With his knife, Rod cut broad notches in the under sides of the braces, near their outer ends, and made matching cuts in the upper surface of the twelve-foot outrigger beam, so that they fitted snugly together. When the outrigger had been lashed to the braces with fiber rope, the whole contrivance was as firm and strong as if it had been built in one piece.

"It will be easier to carry now," grinned Kokua. "Lift and see."

Each boy grasped a cross-brace close to the hull and they picked the canoe up without difficulty. The outrigger balanced the dugout, and the round, three-inch braces offered a good hold.

"We'll have to take her apart to let her down the cliff," said Rod, "but it shouldn't be very hard to carry her that far. What about paddles—and a mast and sail?"

Kokua nodded thoughtfully. "Paddles," he said, "will give us plenty of *pilikia*—trouble. But I have a plan."

He went off to the rocky outcrop where they had killed the goat and when he returned he had several sharp stones of different sizes. Patiently he began chipping and shaping them into wedges.

"Go and get one of the logs we used for rollers," he told Rod. "The biggest one. If we can split it we can make the blades for our paddles."

Rod, used to more civilized implements, was surprised to see how well the stone wedges worked. After two or three bad starts, Kokua succeeded in driving one into the end of the ten-inch log and starting a narrow split along the straight grain of the wood. With care he selected a smaller wedge and hammered it into the crevice. Striking first one and then the other with a heavy stone, he gradually widened the split and started another, an inch away from the first. After an hour of painstaking work the log fell apart, and a few minutes later Kokua had split off a thin slab, big enough to make two service-able paddle blades.

Now it was Rod's turn to show his skill. With his knife he began smoothing the slab, cutting it into two equal lengths and rounding off the ends into a roughly oval shape. The handles were made of straight sticks of *kohala*. When Rod had bored holes in the blades with the point of his knife, they bound the shafts in place with more fiber cord.

There was a thwart across the hull of the canoe, just forward of amidships, and a two-inch hole had been made in its center by the natives who had built it. This hole, and a chock cut into the wood of the bottom directly beneath, were obviously intended for stepping a mast.

"You think there's enough o' this boat canvas left to make us a sail?" Rod asked. He spread the tattered sail-cloth out on the grass and looked at Kokua inquiringly.

"Perhaps," the Island boy replied. "Not a very big sail, but it will help if we get a fair wind."

"I figured we could use the boom, here, for a mast," Rod continued. The boys had long since brought the wreckage from the whale-boat up to the shack, and now it appeared they might have use for it.

Kokua got a long, limber stick for a spar and they

started rigging their craft. The boom fitted the mast hole as if it had been made for it. They cut away the ragged parts of the sail and secured one edge to the lateen spar with lashings of coconut fiber. There was even a small rusty pulley which they fastened to the masthead and used with the remnant of the sheet rope to make a halyard for raising and lowering the sail.

"She's shipshape now," Rod grinned, rubbing his hands. "When do we start?"

Kokua shook his head. "There are still many things to do," he said. "We must have food and water. Maybe two days. Maybe three."

Impatient to begin the voyage, Rod scoffed at the idea, but it turned out that Kokua was right. All the next day he cooked and pounded *poi,* storing it in gourds. Then he went to work on a water-bag. Luckily they had saved the skin of the goat. With a bone needle and ravelings from the discarded rags of sail-cloth he began sewing the edges of the skin together. To make the bag water-tight, the seams had to be lapped and folded, and it was a long, difficult job. At last, on the evening of the second day, he turned the bag inside out and filled it at the spring, hanging it on a pole inside the shack.

"If it is empty in the morning we know it is no good," he said, "and we must start over."

Rod could hear the slow drip of the water from the bag that night as he lay on his mat and tried to sleep. It was a depressing sound. He wondered if they would ever get off—if he would ever listen to white men's talk and wear civilized clothes again—if he would ever see Mahina Kea.

At that point he must have drowsed off, for the next thing he knew Kokua was shaking him awake. Sitting up, he looked first at the goatskin bag. It still looked plump and well filled.

Kokua caught his glance and chuckled. "Only a little water leaked out," he said. "Get up *wikiwiki*—we can go today."

They carried the canoe down the slope through the palm grove and set it down by the top of the cliff. There they untied the lashings and removed the outrigger. Early that morning Kokua had been up into the jungle. He had brought down two more long lianas which he now proceeded to tie around the bow and stern of the canoe. They eased the hull over the edge and let it down slowly till they felt the weight come to rest on the sand. Kokua slid down the vine rope, untied the lianas from the canoe and waited while Rod let down the outrigger, mast and sail. Then they both returned to the shack for breakfast.

The Hawaiian boy looked up at the towering

cliffs that walled the valley and his face was sober. "I have been here a long time," he said. "It is a good place—the Kalalau. I have had a good life here and it makes my heart a little sad to leave it. Some day we will come back, you and I. This is our valley."

Rod could understand the young Kanaka's feeling. The wild grandeur of the Kalalau had touched him too. He spent a full minute drinking in its beauty before he turned back to the practical present.

"Come on," he said. "Time to get going."

They finished eating, wrapped their supply of food carefully and refilled the water-bag. Then, carrying their weapons and provisions, they went down to the cliffs by the sea once more. Five minutes later they stood on the narrow beach, with all their possessions gathered about them.

The outrigger was soon lashed to the canoe and they carried it down so that its prow was in the edge of the waves before loading it. The mast was stepped but they left the sail furled. As Kokua pointed out, the hardest and most dangerous part of their task would be getting out through the surf. That would take skillful paddling and the sail would only be a hindrance.

The trade wind blew steadily from the northeast, sending the big breakers angling in across the reef.

Even from the shore they looked formidable enough. Rod, estimating their chances, knew the canoe might be smashed to pieces on the coral, but he welcomed the prospect of action. Once they were over, their voyage would really begin.

He waded out and climbed over the gunwale, crouching in the bow with his paddle ready. Kokua gave a shout, pushed the canoe out till it cleared the sand, and sprang into the stern.

"Now!" he cried. "Paddle hard!"

XVIII

ROD DROVE the oval blade through the water, picking up the swift beat from Kokua's panting voice. The first roller hit them and cold spray drenched the white boy's naked chest. He laughed exultantly and paddled all the harder.

They were close to the line of the reef now and the waves looked mountain high. One of them caught the canoe a little abeam and tipped it till the outrigger lifted clear of the water. But Kokua's steering brought the bow around before the next wave struck and they rode it without mishap. The Kanaka boy waited till a series of big ones had rolled past, watching the turbulent water over the reef with a practiced eye.

"Now!" he yelled at last.

Rod put everything he had into the next few strokes. The canoe shot forward, lifted its nose high on a sea that was just ready to break, and glided smoothly down the other side. Looking over his shoulder, Rod saw the cruel teeth of the coral behind them. They had crossed the reef in safety.

Kokua steered straight out from the shore for another mile. Then he swung the bow of the canoe to starboard and headed northeast, so that their course lay parallel with the coast. They were paddling directly into the wind now. It was hard work, and their progress seemed painfully slow to Rod, but the feeling of freedom was strong in him. Their staunch little craft was buoyant and handled well. Even the calking they had done with coconut fiber was a success. The only water entering the hull was spray from the wave crests.

On their right the high cliffs still loomed without a break. After an hour's paddling Kokua pointed to a narrow, steep-sided valley cutting back into the heights of the *pali*. "Hanakoa," he said. And when they had covered a few more miles he indicated still another valley, calling it "Hanakapiai."

It was past noon when they rounded a blunt head-land and swung due east. "Up there," said the Kanaka boy, pointing with his paddle, "is the fire cliff. For many years, whenever the Kauai people wanted to hold a big feast, they have come to that place. The cliff is very high, as you can see. And a strong wind blows upward from the bottom to the top. At night, when a burning torch is thrown down from the cliff it hangs in the air and then goes up again. It is a strange thing to see, and very beautiful."

Following the coast, they bore southeastward now, and were able to use the sail. Kokua held the sheet and steered, while Rod kept his paddle deep over the side to act as a lee-board. He was able to give more attention to the shoreline. The mountain ridges were farther back from the beach at this point, and there were green fields and forests in the lowlands between. He got a glimpse into the mouths of two long, deep valleys that sloped upward for miles into the lofty middle of the island. "Wainiha" and "Lumahai," Kokua called them.

Ahead of them Rod saw a rounded bay open up to the southward. It was a pretty spot, with a crescent of white beach running along the curve of the bay for a mile or more. There were groves of palms, their fronds waving in the breeze, and a cluster of native huts beside a small, shining river.

"We will stop here for the night," said Kokua. "This is Hanalei."

Half a dozen young Islanders were playing in the surf and two of the boys swam out to meet the canoe. They were like fish in the water, lithe and tireless. The overhand stroke they used in swimming was a source of constant surprise to Rod, who knew only the clumsy breast stroke he had learned as a child.

"Who are you?" they asked. "And where do you come from?"

"I am Kokua," said the boy at the helm of the canoe. "This is Lok. We come from the valley of Kalalau and are on our way to the Kona side. Where are your chiefs and elders? They should give us proper greeting."

"They have seen you," grinned one of the swimmers. "When your sail came past the point, the women went to prepare food. Listen—you can hear the drums now."

The two young Kanakas held onto the outrigger and swam alongside while Rod let down the sail and unstepped the mast.

A few moments later the canoe was driving in through the surf. They ran it high on the sand and climbed out just as the head of a procession of villagers emerged from the palm grove. Kokua had been careful to keep his feather cape dry under a *lauhala* mat. Now he shook out the folds and draped it over his shoulders. Its colors glowed in the afternoon sun. Even Rod was impressed by the magnificence of his companion's appearance.

To the rhythmic beat of hand drums the line of brown-skinned natives came down the beach. A tall, paunchy man—evidently the village chief—led the way. He, too, wore a ceremonial cape of feathers, but it looked dingy and moth-eaten by comparison with Kokua's.

"Aloha!" the leader called loudly, and Kokua returned the greeting. In a dignified speech the chief inquired politely about the strangers' health, hoped they had enjoyed a pleasant voyage, and extended the poor hospitality of Hanalei.

Kokua replied in the same stilted phrases, thanking him for being so generous to humble wayfarers like themselves. All the while he was throwing out his chest and strutting in his finery, so that Rod had to smile in spite of himself.

The moment the formalities were over, the stiff line of villagers broke and the boys were surrounded by a laughing, friendly crowd. Questions were thrown at them so fast that Rod was hard put to answer them in his halting Hawaiian. They seemed amazed that anybody had survived the terrors of

the supposedly inaccessible valley and escaped.
Kokua didn't belittle his own exploits, but when he
came to tell of Rod's adventures he really let his
imagination go.

The Yankee blushed under his tan as the story
unfolded. Kokua told how Rod had come all the way
from *Melika,* the far-away island where the sun
rose; how he had hunted whales in one of the great
sailing-canoes of the white man; how the entire ship
had been devoured by a whale at one gulp, and only
he of all the crew had fought his way out of the
terrible jaws. Finally he described Rod's epic swim—
"as many leagues as from Kauai to Oahu"—and how
they had met on the beach of Kalalau.

The natives regarded the young *haole* with awe.
Far removed from any seaport, some of them had
never had a close view of a white man before. They
fingered his sheath knife curiously and marveled at
his blue eyes and brown hair.

The sun had set when they were called to the *luau.*
First they were taken to a grass-thatched hut where
fresh mats had been laid on the cleanly swept earth
floor. Bowls of water were supplied so that they
could wash before the feast. Then the village head
man escorted them to an open space in the palm
grove where the food was spread on the ground. He
placed one of the boys on either side of him and they

squatted cross-legged while the rest of the men took their seats according to age and rank.

Besides the inevitable *poi,* there were fish, both cooked and raw, a succulent roast pig, yams and baked bananas, coconuts, papayas and several other kinds of fruit. They ate with great ceremony and for a long time. There were no tools except their fingers. Meat was torn from the roast pig and held in both hands. No sooner was a *poi* bowl empty than the women hurried to refill it.

The stout chief kept on eating with a hearty appetite long after Rod was so full he could hardly move. Out of politeness the boy tried to give the appearance of enjoying every mouthful, but he took smaller and smaller nibbles and chewed each one as long as possible.

At last the meal was ended. They had eaten the final courses by torchlight. Now the space in the middle of the circle was cleared and the flickering flames shone on brown bodies as the dancing began. A native flute piped softly and a drum gave the rhythm. Half a dozen young girls in long *ti*-leaf skirts and flowery *leis* sang a song, swaying to the music and illustrating the words with motions of their hands. They were graceful enough, but Rod's mind strayed back to another night and another *hula* he had seen. He wished he could be back in Oahu.

The music changed to a faster beat and the men stirred themselves. Around the circle they began a grunting chant, bending backward and forward in time with the drum. Then three or four of the younger ones sprang up and started to dance. Kokua was among them, his bright cape flying as he leaped and postured. Each young man picked up a spear which he brandished about his head while he panted the phrases of the war chant.

The dancing went on for close to an hour and when it ended the youths were exhausted, their bodies gleaming with sweat. Kokua flung himself down beside Rod with a grin.

"After a *luau,*" he gasped, "that is good. I could almost eat again."

They had a swim in the river before bedtime, and Rod slept soundly in the guest house provided for them. In the morning they said grateful good-byes to the people of Hanalei and paddled out of the bay while the sun was just coming over the palms.

All forenoon they were working to windward and the sail was of no use. They skirted a low, rocky coast, where the jungle came down close to the shore. If there were any villages among the trees they saw no sign of them. Then, about mid-day, the canoe passed a point of rocks and beyond it the coastline took a bend to the southward. They were able to raise the mast and make a reach of it with the wind on their port beam.

They sighted several canoes fishing outside a small bay where Kokua said there was a village called Moloaa. Farther southward a mountain range approached the coast again, and at its seaward end the Kanaka boy pointed out one of the wonders of the island.

"Look," he said. "This you have never seen. There is a hole in the mountain." And sure enough, Rod could see daylight through an opening just below the peak.

Toward sunset they put into Anahola Bay and camped under the palms that fringed the beach. After the enormous meal of the previous evening, neither of them wanted any more lavish entertainment, and the spot they chose was distant from any village. They ate simply from the provisions they had brought with them. For an hour or more afterward they sat by their little fire and Kokua told Rod stories of the Menehunes.

Long ago, he said, the island of Kauai was inhabited by these little people. They were less than half the size of an ordinary man but very strong. Unlike the Kanakas, who came to the island and conquered them, the Menehunes loved to work as much as to play. They usually slept in the daytime and toiled in the dark. And in a single night they performed tremendous tasks. The big fishpond of Alakoko, near Nawiliwili was one of the things they had built, carrying rocks all the way from the Hoary Head Mountains and piling them into a jetty that dammed off part of the Huleia stream. Perhaps their most famous engineering feat was the "Menehune ditch" at Waimea. It brought water down from the hills in a stone flume, built along the side of a cliff.

Kokua thoroughly believed in the little men. Even now, he said, some of them might be watching from the darkness of the palm grove. As he pointed out with some logic, no Hawaiian had the skill or the energy to do such jobs as he had described. So there must be Menehunes.

They got an early start next morning and bowled along down the coast with the sail drawing full. By noon they had passed the mouth of Wailua River and were off Hanamaulu Bay.

"Not far now to Nawiliwili Harbor," said Kokua. "I have many friends there."

An hour later they rounded Ninini Point and headed into a deep, irregular estuary. There was hardly enough wind to fill the ragged sail, once they were under the lee of the shore. Rod unstepped the mast and they paddled the remaining mile to the head of the bay. Kokua had draped his feather cape over his shoulders in order to cut a dashing figure. He pointed ahead.

"There's the village," he said. "And you can see people already coming down to the beach."

Rod's eyes were fixed on something else. Moored a short distance from the shore was a small two-masted schooner. Her cordage was slack and her furled sails were dingy. The white paint on her hull was weathered and peeling. But men were moving aboard her. He could see a net filled with bales and boxes being swung on deck from a lighter. His heart began to beat faster.

"That schooner," he said. "Where do you suppose she's bound?"

"We can ask when we go ashore," Kokua replied. "The head man here is my father's friend. There will be a big *luau* for us tonight."

They ran the canoe in through the low surf and beached it. A dozen boys and young men surrounded them, chattering like magpies. Kokua's cape created all the excitement he could wish, and it was five minutes before the natives stopped exclaiming over it. Finally Rod was able to ask one of them a question.

"The *haole* ship out there," he said, pointing

toward the schooner. "Do you know where it is going?"

"Honolulu," answered the Kanaka. "It will raise its sails before the sun goes down."

The double canoe that served as a lighter had returned to shore, and Rod could see a burly-looking white man talking to its crew on the beach. He left the welcoming crowd that surrounded Kokua and ran toward the other group.

"Are you the cap'n o' that schooner?" he asked breathlessly.

The big white man turned and stared at him. There was little friendliness in his watery blue eyes. Red-faced and slack-jawed, he looked like a man too fond of the bottle.

"An' what if I am?" he grunted.

"I want to get back to Honolulu," Rod explained. "I'm off the whaler *Pelican*. Our boat got smashed by a whale an' I was washed ashore on the north side o' the island."

The man shrugged. "No room in our crew for beachcombers," he said gruffly. "All Kanaka boys." He would have turned away, but Rod laid an urgent hand on his arm.

"I can pay," the boy gulped. "I'll give you a big pearl."

The schooner captain's eyes narrowed. "Hmm," he said. "Let's see it."

Rod fumbled at the little pouch tied to his belt. He got it open and pulled out a pearl which he laid in the skipper's palm. A greedy look came into the man's face as he peered at the gleaming ball.

"Yeah," he said at length. "We'll take ye to Honolulu. Sail in an hour." He pocketed the pearl and swung on his heel.

XIX

THE TRADING schooner *Moana* was as filthy below decks as she was dilapidated above. Rod had been given a bunk aft, in a tiny cabin at the foot of the companion ladder. The mate berthed in a similar cubicle, across the passage, and the captain's cabin occupied the stern.

Rod lay in his narrow bunk and tried to forget the stale, sour smell of dirt that pervaded the place. It had been hard to say good-bye to Kokua. At first the young Islander had been hurt and sulky at his friend's sudden decision to leave. But he had to admit that this might be the only opportunity Rod would have for months. In the end he had thrown his arms around the white boy and wished him well. He had even offered to give him the cape as a present, but Rod refused, promising to visit him on Kauai if ever the chance came his way.

Aboard the schooner he had tried to make friends with the three Kanakas who formed the crew. They were a surly lot, recruited from islands south of the Sandwich group, and their dialect was so different he found it impossible to talk with them except in pidgin English. The fifth man aboard was the mate. Rod had disliked him from the start. He was a stringy little Britisher off the London docks, shifty-eyed and rat-faced. When he gave orders to the crew he cursed steadily in a snarling, cockney voice.

The night wind held steady and the schooner footed along at a good pace. Rod could hear the gurgle and slap of waves under her run, and the sound and the gentle motion lulled him to sleep after a while. His slumber must have been deep, for he did not rouse when the flimsy lock on his cabin door was forced. It was something else that woke him—the touch of a hand on the bare skin of his midriff.

He lay still for a second or two, gathering his wits. The intruder was leaning over him in the dark-ness and he could hear muffled, stealthy breathing.

Again the hand touched him, feeling for the leather pouch at his waist. Rod gathered himself and struck upward with his fist, putting all his force behind it. The blow landed. He felt his knuckles sting with pain as they smashed against bone. There was a gasp from above him and a half-whispered oath. Then Rod whirled over the edge of the berth and grappled with the man.

They fought in silence, straining and heaving in the narrow space between bunk and door. From his size Rod knew his adversary must be the mate. He was small but quick and wiry, and at this kind of fighting he was dangerous. Before the boy could get a firm grip he felt lean fingers clutching his throat and a thumb gouged at his eye socket.

Desperately, Rod brought his knee up and the cockney doubled over with a grunt, loosening his strangle hold. The young whaler struck again with his fist, swinging an uppercut, and by sheer luck it connected. It caught the man flush on the jaw, lifted him off his feet and flung him backward. His head hit the bulkhead with a crash and he lay still.

For a moment Rod stood there panting. He felt of his eye and his bruised knuckles. Finding that no real damage had been done, he hoisted the unconscious mate under the arms, dragged him across the passage and dumped him in his own bunk. When he had closed the door he listened for sounds of movement in the after cabin. He had no more reason to trust the captain than the mate, and he thought the noise of the scuffle must have wakened the beefy skipper. A low-pitched snore reassured him. He went back into his cubbyhole, locked the door again and lay down. For a long time he kept awake, expecting more trouble, but none came. He woke after daylight to find his bag of pearls undisturbed.

Rod saw neither the captain nor the mate when he came on deck. There was an Islander at the wheel and the other two hands sat cross-legged by the foremast-foot, munching bananas. They offered one to the white boy and he made it do for breakfast.

The *Moana* must have logged seven or eight miles an hour through the night, for the mountains of Oahu rose on the port bow. The steersman kept his course far enough offshore to hold the breeze as they ran down the coast. About the middle of the morning they rounded Barber Point and came into the wind, tacking up toward the harbor. It was not until they were a mile from moorings that the skipper appeared. He was rumpled, bleary-eyed and unshaven, and Rod could smell the rum on his breath from twenty feet away.

"Where the devil's Binks?" he growled. "Hey—you lousy limey—roll out here an' bear a hand!"

He stumbled aft again and dragged the protesting mate up the companion.

"I'm sick, Skipper," Binks whined. "Some'ow I fell an' bumped me 'ead, an' it 'urts orful." He sneaked a glance toward Rod but refused to meet the boy's eye. There was malice in him yet, but not much fight.

They worked their way in through the anchored whale-ships and dropped their hook in shoal water a short distance from the docks. The captain ordered his dinghy lowered.

"Come on," he told Rod. "I'll take ye ashore." His manner was more affable now, but his bloodshot eyes were on the little leather sack.

When they landed he took hold of the boy's arm. "Let's go in the tavern yonder," he urged. "I'll buy ye a drink."

Rod jerked loose and faced him. "No, thanks," he said. "I'm due at Mr. MacNair's office. He's a friend of mine."

The red-faced skipper took half a step forward as if he meant to grab the boy again. Then the name Rod had mentioned halted him. "Oh," he said uncertainly. "Well, I'll be seein' ye later."

Perhaps it was because he had been thinking of MacNair's daughter that the shipyard-owner's name had slipped so easily off Rod's tongue. At any rate, his bluff had worked. Now he had to go through with it, for the schooner captain was still watching him speculatively.

He walked along the waterfront toward the yard, paused under a small signboard and knocked on a door.

"Come in," said a voice inside.

Rod opened the door and entered. Not until that moment, when he saw Robert MacNair's amused eyes upon him, had he thought of the way he was dressed. The *lauhala* loincloth was his sole article of apparel.

The man at the table facing him was handsome and clean-shaven. He had laid aside his coat, but his linen shirt was snowy, his trousers of the finest material and his boots well polished. He looked the gentleman he was.

"And what can I do for you, my lad?" he asked politely. There was a pleasant Scotch burr in his voice.

"Thanks, sir, for not taking me for a Kanaka," Rod smiled. "It's a long story, but I've come to you because I heard you well spoken of by Captain Beale, of the *Pelican*. You see, sir, I was one of her crew when we stopped here a few months back."

MacNair's eyebrows went up. "You deserted?" he asked with less warmth in his tone.

"No, sir," Rod replied. "I was cast away. Probably you wouldn't have heard the news, but the *Pelican* lost a boat—the first mate's boat—off Kauai, in September. I was in her. We got fast to a fighting whale that towed us clean out of sight of the ship. It was a good boat, sir. You built it. But when the white whale caught it between his jaws, no wood could stand the bite. As far as I know, every man aboard was killed, except myself."

He paused, his face grim, and MacNair nodded.

"The word got back to us," he said quietly. "Beale spoke another ship a few days after. He was still searching the sea for his men. Go on with your story, laddie."

For nearly an hour, Rod talked. When he finished he laid the bag of pearls on the table.

"I hoped you could help me find a safe place for these," he said. "The skipper of the *Moana* and his cockney mate would both like to get their hands on them."

MacNair snorted. "They've a bad reputation hereabouts," he said. "But I think you'll have nothing to fear from them. We'll take the pearls to the bank. They'll be worth a good bit of money."

He leaned back and studied the boy, an appraising look in his gray eyes. "What would you like to do now?" he asked. "Ship aboard another whaler, I suppose."

"I'm not sure, sir. I've come to like the Islands. If a boy worked hard here, and didn't let the sunshine spoil him, maybe he could make a good life for himself."

MacNair smiled agreement. "I did," he said. "You've picked up enough Hawaiian to be able to talk to the Kanakas. That might help you in finding a place with a good house. Most white men who come out here have trouble with the language for years."

Rod felt his face reddening under the tan but he couldn't help it. He swallowed twice, then blurted out what was in his mind.

"I was thinking, sir," he gulped, "that maybe you could use a strong, willing fellow at the yard. You've been mighty kind and understanding. I'd rather work for you than anybody I know."

The shipbuilder laughed and slapped his thigh. "It's a capital idea," he said. "Until you spoke I hadn't thought of it, but you're just the man for the job. My paymaster was a German chap. He left me last week—ran off to dig for gold in California. If you can add and subtract figures, that's all that's needed. The main thing is to get along with the men—talk their language and understand their happy-go-lucky ways. Dietrich never did. He was too dull and serious."

MacNair got up and came around the table. He held out his hand and grinned.

"I like you," he said frankly. "You've got the right spirit. If you're going to work for me I want to take you home and let you meet my family. But first"—he eyed the ragged loincloth with a smile—"let's go out and buy you some clothes."

There was a good tailor on Queen Street, but it would have taken too long to have a suit measured and made. The shipbuilder took Rod instead to a marine outfitting shop nearer the docks. There he was waited on by the proprietor, and in a few minutes he was attired in white duck pantaloons and a well-made shirt. Next his calloused feet were fitted with socks and squeezed into a pair of boots—the first he had worn since the *Pelican* entered the Pacific.

"Now to the barber's," MacNair chuckled. "Man, you've a shock o' hair that would scare a Fiji Islander."

At last, properly dressed and shorn, the boy was taken to the bank, where his new friend introduced him. With MacNair as his sponsor, he arranged a modest loan, leaving the pearls as security. He felt better when he saw them locked in the big iron safe.

Now that he had money in his pocket he insisted first of all on repaying his employer the amount he had spent for the clothes and the hair-cut.

It was well along in the afternoon now, and Rod was nearly starved. He had eaten nothing that day but the banana given him by the Kanakas. Too shy to mention the fact, he accompanied MacNair back to the yard. There he met the foreman, a tall, raw-boned Yankee from Maine, by the name of Preble. He had learned his shipbuilding at Bath. Though he was cordial enough in a dry, short-spoken way, his shrewd eyes seemed to be sizing Rod up.

"Mr. Bob," he said after a moment, "this boy's hungry."

MacNair looked startled. Then he laughed. "You're right!" he said. "I'd forgotten he was a passenger on the *Moana*. Little enough to eat there, I'll be bound. Come, Rodney. We'll see if we can't hurry supper a bit, up at the house."

They went along the familiar streets, under the monkey-pods and palms and past the hibiscus hedges.

"Honolulu isn't a bad place to live," the Scotchman said. "You miss the snow and the cold sometimes, but there are compensations. We'll see if we can get you a room in a good, clean home. The sailors' boardinghouses along the waterfront are poor quarters for decent folk."

They climbed the Punchbowl and were only a few steps from the driveway of the MacNair mansion when he spoke again, casually. "My wife," he said, with a little smile, "is a Hawaiian lady. I think you'll like her—and my daughter, who's about your age."

Rod bit his lip before he answered. "I—I'm sure I will," he said. And a moment later they were at the door.

*   *   *

He stood on the *lanai,* looking out toward Diamond Head. Mr. MacNair had taken him there and left him for a moment while he went to speak to his wife. There was a trembling in Rod's knees. Everything that had happened since he came ashore was almost too good to be true. He pinched himself to make certain he wasn't dreaming.

Then he heard steps behind him and turned to see the tall, sweet-faced Hawaiian woman he remembered. She held her husband's arm and smiled at the brown boy on the *lanai*.

"My dear," said the shipbuilder, "this is Rodney Glenn, the young man I was speaking of. Rodney—Mrs. MacNair."

Rod bowed in some confusion. He felt painfully awkward and knew that he was blushing. But the next moment she put him at ease.

"It's a pleasure," her soft voice said, "to meet you, Rodney. What an adventure you have had! I hope to hear more about it, but perhaps you would rather wait till our daughter comes home. She went for a ride up the *pali* trail this afternoon. To take a swim," she added, and Rod, looking up quickly, saw a twinkle in her eye.

"Meanwhile," she went on, "I have asked the servants to bring you something to eat."

"Thank you, ma'am," he murmured. And the gratitude he felt was for something more than food.

He took the edge off his hunger with fruit and *poi* while the MacNairs chatted. It was just after the dishes were carried out that he heard hoofbeats in the drive. Then he heard Mahina Kea's voice on the terrace behind him.

"Hello, Mother," she called. "And Dad! You're home early! Oh, I didn't see you had company. I'll go and change."

"That's all right," laughed her father. "Come on up." But Mrs. MacNair shook her head. She went swiftly past Rod and took the girl into the house by another door.

MacNair smiled indulgently. "Just like a woman," he said. "They always have to dress up for guests. Well, that gives us a chance to talk a bit. I asked the banker for a rough appraisal on those pearls of yours, and you're a fairly rich man, Rodney. He can't tell exactly what they're worth till he makes a more careful examination, but he thinks they'd bring at least ten thousand dollars in New York or London. Double that if they're perfectly matched. What would you do with all that money?"

"Save it," said Rod promptly. "I'd have something to put into a business for myself if I make good here."

MacNair chuckled. "That's the talk!" he replied. "It's what I hoped you'd say. Well, here come the ladies."

Rod got to his feet, the blood pounding in his ears. They came out on the *lanai* together.

MacNair had also risen. "I'd like you to meet my little girl, Mahina Kea, Rodney," he was saying.

She looked like a mischievous angel in her graceful white *muumuu*. Demurely she curtsied.

"I'm very happy to meet you, Rodney," she said, with just a trace of huskiness in her voice. "Mother tells me you've been through some terrible experiences. I'm—I'm so glad you're back—I mean safe."

* * *

There is an enchanted hour after sunset when Hawaii is at its loveliest. The soft trade wind rustles the palm fronds in the dusk and the air is filled with the fragrance of a million flowers.

Rodney had long since told the story of his adventures. Now he walked with Mahina Kea in the garden below the terrace. Her warm, slim hand was in his, and her face was radiant even in the semidarkness.

"I knew you'd come back," she said. "I don't know why, but I was certain. Oh, Rod—if I'd known what was happening to you, I don't think I could have stood it!"

"Sometimes," he answered, "I wasn't so sure myself. But I never gave up hoping."

He waited a little while, trying to control the shakiness in his voice. Then he spoke the words that had been in his mind a long time.

"I think," he said, "I've wanted to come back to you ever since we said good-bye. Some day, Mahina Kea, if I get ahead in your father's business—do you suppose—?"

"Yes," she whispered. That was all, but there was a soft light in her eyes. He knew she understood.

Mrs. MacNair called to them from the house and they started up the hill, hand in hand. Suddenly Rod paused and laughed a little.

"It's a funny thing to think of just now," he said, "but I ought to write a letter—two letters. One to my uncle and aunt, to let them know I'm safe. The other to a man in Lenox, Massachusetts. He told me about whaling and about the South Seas. And it's all true—even the white whale, and now—this. I don't know his real name but perhaps he'll get the letter. He's a writer fellow. Told me to call him Ishmael."

THE END